Vice

A P Bateman

Text © A P Bateman
2023

This book is a work of fiction and any character resemblance to persons
living or dead is purely coincidental. Some locations may have been
changed; others are fictitious.

Parts of this book was first published in 2017 as 'Hell's Mouth'. Many
locations, characters, plot lines and subplots have changed.

Facebook: @authorapbateman
Website: www.apbateman.com

For the other three in "The Four Family"
Thank you...

Also by A P Bateman

Stone Cold

The DCI Grant Series

Vice

Taken

Standalone Novels

Never Go Back

Novellas

The Perfect Murder?

Atonement

(an Alex King short story)

Chapter One

"Y ou'll know when you see it, son. It will all become clear. And I trust that you will know what to do..."

Those had been his final words. Not on the man's deathbed. Nothing as dramatic as that. But he had been adamant. He had told him half a story and given him the means and time and opportunity to discover the other half. It had been typical of Maitland. He had not wanted the man's opinion jaded in any way. Simply given him the time and the place. The rest was for him to discover. As last words went, it had piqued his interest.

Grant put down the telephone. He would know who his new boss would be soon enough. He felt numb at the news, but death was an old and constant companion. He had spent enough time with it, knew the processes of grief only too well. In his darkest hours, he did not fear death, nor shied from its path. Outside forces had contributed, but ultimately death was a face he no longer feared to stare into. Occasionally he goaded it, stared coldly and dared it to make its move. It had made for a flat line in both career and love. He was unbreakable. He was uncontrollable. Untameable. And that meant that with the replacement of his long-time boss, he would most likely be unemployable. He was a crisis man. The man you wanted on board when the toughest choices had to be made, when it counted. But crisis men were like tethered animals. They only truly lived when they were free.

Fifty-nine days...

The longest period since the clock turned back and the marker read zero. His heart fluttered and his stomach tensed. He could feel a sudden rush in his chest cavity as the blood surged quicker through his veins. He started to ball his fists as he walked out of Maitland's study and into the lounge. Maitland had kept a crystal decanter of Haig single malt whisky in the study and the temptation was behind him now. He had looked at the decanter, its amber contents glistening in the late afternoon sun which shone brightly through the windows. The proximity of the water had seemed to intensify the light, given it an added quality of candescence he seldom saw, or perhaps ever noticed in London.

The entire south wall of the lounge had been replaced by glass doors and the view spoke for itself. The creek was almost at high-tide and the water was the deepest blue, pooling to black in the shadows of the trees on the other side. It was late summer, the final weeks where the next front of cold weather spelled the end of the season and the beginning of autumn.

The body of water this far up the creek wasn't popular with paddle boarders or kayakers. It was shallow and held on to the flat bed of mud and grass for all but three-quarter tide. Lower down the creek at Point, less than a mile distant, there would be hordes of children, clad in brightly coloured wetsuits, jumping off the jetty into the deep water. There would be kayaks and other craft paddling through the moorings as the last weeks of ideal boating conditions were exploited, and sailors started preparing their boats for hauling out of the water for the long winter months ahead.

Across the water lay an old wooden jetty. It was all but hidden from view by a large fallen tree which must have become snagged, or sucked into the mud, because it hadn't moved for the entire week. Each time the tide partially submerged it but still it did not move. The absence of leaves would indicate that it had not fallen this summer. It looked to have been there for years. Perhaps it had taken root in the mud. Grant did not know about such things, lacked the care to *Google* it, but he reasoned that it was not in the way of the tiny jetty, nor the rest of the river, so its presence was of no consequence.

Grant stepped into the open doorway and leaned on the warm glass. Birds skimmed the surface of the water, and a species of black and white bird was ducking down repeatedly and reappearing twenty or thirty feet further down the creek each time. It seemed to be following a line. Grant figured there was food there. Perhaps shrimp. But what did he know? He couldn't have said whether it was a cormorant or a duck.

He stepped outside and felt the sun on his face. It was hovering between late afternoon and early evening. Another hour until dusk. The sun was warm, and the water looked inviting enough to swim in. He put the thought out of his mind. A bad experience, a trauma he supposed, had left him with little desire to swim. It was too soon. The proximity of the creek had left him feeling anxious, but he reasoned he had control over it. He just had to stay on dry land. He had been a champion swimmer a lifetime ago, and a water polo player at university. The sport had shaped him, broadened his shoulders, trimmed his waist and left him with an athletic build, even when he no longer trained. It saddened him that another part of his life was over, and he was left with nothing but regret and distant memories. He seemed to be following a pattern throughout life. Or maybe it was just the way it went when you got older, crossed into the uncertainty of middle age.

The warmth of the sun did nothing to lift his spirits. The call had been swift, but mainly because he was at a loss what to say. What did you say to a woman whose husband has just died? Grant counted Maitland as one of his closest friends, even if he had been his boss since he arrived in the department. He hadn't known the man had been suffering with cancer; wouldn't even have guessed. But that was what the man had been like. Maitland wouldn't want pity or sorrow or awkward silences in a conversation. It struck Grant that the man's wife hadn't known either, although it didn't surprise him of the man. He was tough and would want to be remembered that way. He hadn't even looked sick, but there were a few tell-tale signs upon reflection. Weight loss, pallor, unexplained absences from work. But all handled like typical Maitland. *Diet. Need a bloody holiday. Busy on an investigation, hush-hush stuff.* He wondered whether Maitland had helped himself along, found a way out before the suffering reduced him as a man. He would have known a few methods that would not have been obvious. Or maybe he had got his wife to help him, and she was a little off during the conversation because of fear or guilt or regret. He made a note to put his oar in if he heard anything on the grapevine, anything to give her an easier ride. *If* he had a job to go back to.

Grant needed a beer. A cold glass in the setting sun, a

toast to his departed friend, his mentor and his boss. Just one bottle. Frosted, quenching, but wholly unforgiving. There were some bottles of something German in the back of the fridge. He could imagine the sound of the bottle top spinning off and hitting the polished granite counter, hear the fizz of the beer as it frothed, see the tiny bubbles pop and burst in the air above the rim.

He could taste it...

Before he knew it, he was running. He kicked open the wooden gate, his pace barely slowing as he joined the well-trodden path along the bank of the creek. He hadn't run for more than two-months. Not since before his accident. Or incident. Incident would best describe it. He shook his head, clearing the memory. Focus. Focus on the pace, his breath, his stride. Think about anything else but the bottle, anything else but the empty bottle that invariably always led to another.

Fifty-nine days...

Grant knew the problem. He had been inactive for too long. He needed a crutch. Something to take a hold of him, his mind and body. His soul. Maitland had seen that. He had known what a task it would be for him to take a full two-months away from his desk, his patch. He had given him the chance of a break, but one with purpose. One he was most suited to. But what? Grant cursed the man for being so bloody cryptic. There had been the newspaper clippings from the national press and a good deal of reports from the *West Briton* when the nationals moved swiftly onto the next story. And there had been the copies of the reports he had pulled. Maitland had clout, that much was obvious. He had increased Grant's leave and postponed his psychoanalyst programmes after the initial inquiry. He knew Grant needed something practical to concentrate on, and no amount of therapy was going to change what had happened. He also knew that Grant hid a condition that would have cost him his job. Analysts had a habit and ability to unearth more than was good for their patient.

Maitland had been the one person Grant could count on, and now the man was dead. And with it, Grant's hopes of continuing with the investigation. Without Maitland, it was as good as dead in the water.

Dead in the water...

Grant stopped running and stared at the water. The tide was moving rapidly, like a walking escalator at an airport. There was a piece of driftwood coming in with it and it gave a sense of perspective of how fast the tide was moving. He knew it went out faster. Or he might have made that up. Either way, it seemed obvious to him that the pull would be stronger than the push. Especially in calm conditions with no storm surge.

He watched a medium-sized fishing boat coming in. It was powered by an in-built diesel engine that sounded as if it had seen better days - around fifty-years ago - and housed a substantial cabin on the foredeck. Grant could see two men at the helm. One rolled a cigarette and the other raised his finger, covered his left nostril and shot-gunned his nose, a spray of snot hitting the water. They glanced at him, but Grant looked away and from the corner of his eye they both looked uninterested as they piloted the boat around an exposed mud bank and onwards up the creek. The rear section of the deck was stacked with two types of lobster or crab pots. Rounded ones that looked as if they were made from wicker and larger square metal cages. Huge coils of rope seemed to pack them in, and there were plastic crates staked alongside.

Maitland had been quite specific. Tonight, was the

second time and date in the letter. Grant had missed the first time, last week. He had met up with a woman that he had initially met on his first night in the local pub. He felt bad missing the time and date, but Maitland could be a dick sometimes. Grant had felt obliged to come down to Cornwall, as though it were an order rather than a suggestion, although he had been quite entitled to his time off from work, considering what had happened. This had been Maitland's family home, or at least one of them. His commander had referred to it as the *Hemingway House*, because of its likeness to the writer Ernest Hemingway's home in Key West, Florida. Strangely, it did not look out of place, predominately because of the types of houses which had sprung up over the past decade or so. This was an affluent area, one of second homes and holiday lets, and the plots were being bought up and old houses knocked down in favour of newly built chrome, glass and expensively weathered oak constructions. *Hemingway House* was modern, but chic. It added a touch of class to the area, where only money remained.

The date had gone well. They had picked up where they had left off, but without the cluster of regulars heckling them at the local pub. They had met for cocktails in Truro and gone on to eat at a favourable Italian chain restaurant. Grant had stuck rigidly to the crutch of his car. If he was driving, it was socially unacceptable to drink, especially within their age group. Besides, a taxi back to Point and Loe Creek beyond was a ludicrous proposition to most. The myriad of roads, the hills and narrow turnings to get out to the creek. Situated past Mylor, a taxi would cost almost as much as the meal itself. In his mind, at least. With that, the cocktails had been 'mocktails' and a simple lime and soda went well with the meal instead of chilled Italian beer.

There may be a talk about his drinking later, but this wasn't suitable for first date conversation. The gap in both age and dynamic had taken a downwards turn when Mary had suggested a club. Grant had just hit forty and it showed in his panic at the prospect of dancing in a loud and crowded club with a thirty-year-old who would pass for early twenties. The sincerity and confidence of the idea was put into context, when they arrived and discovered the club had been closed for a considerable length of time. It seemed to Grant that Mary had felt a little foolish about being in the dark concerning the closure of the nightclub, and along with snippets of conversation throughout the night he thought that she did not get out as much. And that meant there had to be a reason. Something she had not disclosed, something she had purposely avoided. It was the detective in him. The role never left him. Not even when it had cost him his wife and child. But that hadn't been the only reason.

Fifty-nine days...

He glanced at his watch. The sun was now below the furthest-most headland towards Restronguet Point. The timing would be right. He turned and jogged back to the house. There was the occasional dog walker, who said, "Good evening..." or nodded a greeting. He could not get used to it. People *spoke* to strangers down here. In London they'd call the police, because you would clearly have escaped from some sort of institution if you behaved in such a manner.

The boat's rough-sounding engine belied its speed and Grant had to run a good pace to catch up with it as he rounded the point and drew close to Loe Creek. The *Hemingway House* looked as splendid as ever, but the light was low here and he knew that there may not be enough light to watch what happened next. Breathless and tentative, he ran through the doors and into the lounge. Maitland had appreciated ornithology and kept a pair of Zeiss binoculars on the bookshelf next to the glass doors. Grant picked them up. They were a good magnification and a series of symbols on the side of the frame indicated they were suitable for low light conditions, as well as their significant degree of magnification and width of angle. There were no lights on in the house and he stood a few feet back to remain invisible. He raised the glasses and watched the boat as it manoeuvred around the fallen tree then throttled backwards and suddenly disappeared. Now he could see how significant the tree was. There were enough branches to disrupt the silhouette of the vessel and combined with the trees on the shoreline and the growing darkness the boat was out of sight. Grant knew this was what Maitland had meant for him to see. The time, the date, the location. All reliant on the tides and time of dusk. But why? Why would a commander in Special Branch have an interest in this? These men could be fishing or poaching from the nearby estate. There were deer all over that headland. Grant had heard gunshots the night before. But this was the country, not London and nobody seemed to bat an eyelid. He had mentioned it at the local pub, and one of the men at the bar had offered him a rabbit the next time he went out.

Grant supposed that the men on the boat could be bringing in cigarettes and alcohol to escape duty. A questionable activity, and one that no police officer would ignore, but merely a tip-off to the local constabulary would be action enough. Why had Maitland seen fit to offer his house to him? What wasn't Grant seeing? He kept his eyes on the area where the boat had moored. It was much darker now and he could no longer see the tree, and only guessed at where the boat was, but he could make out a figure on the jetty. One of the men for sure. Then, two more figures. No, three. Varying sizes, perhaps indicating either different sexes or ages. Grant closed his eyes for a moment. There were the reports, the newspaper articles. He opened his eyes and pressed them closer to the binoculars in vain. He strained his eyes, moved the focus. He took them away and checked the magnification. There was a dial. He was on seven and it went to ten. Perfect. There was a switch on the top of the frame simply marked 'on' and 'off'. It had to be better if you turned it on. He raised them and looked again. For a fleeting moment he saw a figure looking back at him, a set of binoculars raised. The light in the room illuminated him, cast his silhouette in the open doorway. He visibly jumped and cursed his incompetence.

"What on earth are you doing?" Mary asked as she walked in carrying two brown paper bags and an aroma of Chinese food wafting along with her.

"Switch off the light!" he yelled. She looked at him incredulously. She was not accustomed to being shouted at. Either that, or she had been once and had now drawn a line in the sand. He suspected the latter. Something about the resolute way she ignored his command. "The light, the bloody light! Turn it off!" he yelled again. She tutted loudly and switched the light off as he raised the binoculars. The man on the distant jetty had gone. Grant felt the tiny hairs rise on the nape of his neck. He had a sinking feeling that he had witnessed something that someone would go to great lengths to make sure he hadn't.

Chapter Two

Eight weeks earlier
London

DI Grant studied the photo in his lap. He checked the man walking towards him, there was no beard, and his hair was cropped short instead of his usual long, greasy strands that bordered on dreadlocks. The man was thinner, too. Drawn, gaunt. Was it him? He'd been this close before. Sat opposite him for three days of questioning. Sat across the courtroom from him for two-months during the trial. He'd been forced to watch the man walk away then. But not now. Not today. With just ten paces between them, he folded the photograph so that only the eyes remained. He focused for a moment, then stared directly into the man's face. Two seconds, and he was gone. Past the car and walking away with his back to the wing mirror. It was all he needed. Those eyes were the same. Like the eyes of a shark. Dark and emotionless.

He lifted the radio, just enough to capture his voice, not raising it in full view for the rest of the people crossing the bridge to see. "Control, Bravo Delta Two," he said, clearly and in control of his emotions despite the building adrenalin within. "Positive ID, repeat, positive ID."

"Bravo Delta Two, confirmed, positive ID. All units, standby, standby. Sit rep on SCO19?"

"SCO19. Four minutes."

"Speed up."

"Control. Bravo Delta Two, I'm in position," Grant interjected when the net was clear.

"Denied."

"Control, I'm right here!" Grant snapped. "He's got the look; he's bloody well praying as he walks! Whatever he's going to do, he's going to do it now!"

"Denied, Grant. Wait out!"

Shaved, hair trimmed, washed and presentable for *Paradise*, wide-eyed and mouthing a prayer, almost in a meditative state. It didn't get more imminent than that. Grant opened the door of the van and swung his wiry six-foot frame out onto the pavement. He kept the radio down by his side. He could see the man from behind. He had a shuffle going on, like he was rocking to a beat as he walked. Which indeed he was. But it went with the chant he was mouthing, nothing musical, merely the constant reciting of a near-silent prayer.

Ahead of the man, Grant could see the gathering of children. A school outing, the children holding leaflets, gathered around a brass plaque. William Wordsworth's poem of Westminster Bridge. The teacher leading the talk was standing with her back to the river. Teaching assistants and keen parents making up the numbers stood nearby, cordoning off the children as they watched and listened.

The teacher had a sheet of paper in her hands, and she cleared her throat before speaking. Had Grant been closer, he would have heard:

"Earth has not anything to show more fair:
Dull would he be of soul who could pass by
A sight so touching in its majesty:
This City now doth like a garment wear
The beauty of the morning; silent, bare,
Ships, towers, domes, theatres, and temples lie
Open unto the fields, and to the sky;
All bright and glittering in the smokeless air.
Never did sun more beautifully steep
In his first splendour valley, rock, or hill;
Ne'er saw I, never felt, a calm so deep!
The river glideth at his own sweet will:
Dear God! the very houses seem asleep;
And all that mighty heart is lying still!"

The teacher continued to talk, and the children listened. Passers-by paused and nodded. The bridge had seen a terrorist atrocity when self-styled terrorist and Islamic extremist Khalid Masood killed four and injured more than fifty people when he drove down the pavement at over seventy-miles-per-hour and crashed his hire car outside The Palace of Westminster and callously murdered PC Keith Palmer on 22nd March 2017.

Grant was sure the bridge was about to see another attack. They had been lucky with the intelligence. Social media was being monitored constantly, but Abhim Jafri had been careless. He had not friended a person, but a picture, a story, a social invention. He had requested the friendship of a person who didn't exist, from a computer and server in a place that did. GCHQ. A team of operators trawling the net for an 'in'. The software and telephone recognition system, known as ECHELON, had picked up Jafri six months previous, and not just one, but three times. Jafri was targeted and several attempts to insert a cyber-spy into his network were rebuked. But then came the break the intelligence operatives at Cheltenham had been waiting for, Jafri sent a friend request to a ghost account, and they had him. They didn't pounce, keeping him waiting a week to be accepted, but then it was on. That person who appealed to him was ingeniously inserted into his internet usage. Someone who came up as a suggested friend because of other ghost accounts he had as so-called friends. Jafri could see the posts, did not know that the two-hundred friends the ghost account displayed were all GCHQ accounts and 'legends' and it was not long before the extremist rhetoric played to Abhim Jafri had hooked him in. Open messages were sent, with each end describing what they wanted to do and achieve in the name of Allah. Human rights lawyers would argue entrapment and coercion, but the accounts were filtering enough 'real' people, and GCHQ were confident, that with help and cooperation from MI5, that they could sever the line and keep Jafri's social media trail natural to all who would later inspect it. Besides, they were the country's communication intelligence service and were protected by joint intelligence and the Terrorism Act. The truth was, the extremists were there, they sometimes needed bolstering and nurturing, encouraging even, to step up and commit their act of terrorism. Better it was the intelligence services than an extremist cleric or Imam where the trail would remain undetected.

As an officer of Special Branch, DI Grant was part of the joint operation with MI5, working on the intel handed over by GCHQ – a non-field operational service. The role of Special Branch in an operation such as this, was to make MI5's arrest. SCO19, the specialist armed police unit of highly trained officers was on hand to provide armed support. The arrest would be a hard stop - armed officers surrounding Jafri and eliminating the threat. Grant and his team would read the rights, so to speak and MI5 would accompany Special Branch officers in the interview. Only it hadn't worked out that way. Jafri had given the surveillance team the slip, the officers were dispersed all over the city and had only just relocated Jafri by chance. Grant had cut through the traffic by a devious route and made it to the bridge. SCO19 were in transit from what was initially confirmed as the target area, a shopping centre situated on the other side of the river. Now that Grant had got the second eyes-on and confirmed a positive ID, the target made sense. Jafri was a former work colleague of Khalid Masood and Westminster Bridge seemed a fitting location to rein terror once more.

Grant broke into a jog, keeping his eyes on Jafri. His pace slowed and he fumbled with his jacket. It was a hot day, but the jacket had been noted, profiling had indicated that Jafri would be operating alone. They knew there would be something under the jacket. Jafri's browser history was of suicide vests and bomb-making. SCO19 had been made aware of this in the briefing. Standard operating procedure of taking shots at the target's central body mass was being changed by the advent of suicide vests. Israeli officers now only attempted head shots. The practise was becoming the same for British forces. They would ultimately have to make their own call, but the officers had each come onto their shift knowing that if they needed to fire upon Jafri, then extreme prejudice protocols would be required.

Jafri stopped at the group of school children. Grant was sprinting now. Jafri pulled off his jacket to reveal a vest, but this was no suicide vest. There were two short-handled khanjar knives, or Arabian daggers, strapped to the man's back. The vest was a bullet-proof or stab-proof vest, and slashes made in the top layer of material acted as sheaths for the khanjar knives. He drew them swiftly, both blades were approximately fourteen inches long, curved and had wickedly pointed tips. Jafri slashed them through the air and the first person, a parent or teaching assistant, fell to the floor, partially decapitated. He did not wait to look at his handiwork; merely kept slashing. The full horror of what was happening took moments for the onlookers to comprehend, in which time, Jafri had felled another adult and a small child. People screamed and ran in both directions, and an oncoming crowd soon blocked Grant's view of the terrible scene. Grant pushed the terrified people out of the way as he barged onwards running against the crowd.

Jafri had a group of children cornered at a buttress. There was terror on their faces and the sound of screaming came from every direction. Amid the chaos, a teenaged boy had stopped walking and was filming the scene on his phone. His presence seemed surreal, voyeuristic in the extreme. Grant could hear approaching sirens and the noise of the screaming was dying down as people ran far enough away to safety. He reached the first casualty, but he could already see that they were dead. The next body was that of a child, equally as far gone as the first body. No hope.

Jafri stood above a woman who was sobbing and crawling into the road. She was the teacher who had recited the poem, and she was bleeding heavily from slashes to her arms, legs and shoulders. She looked to have put up a fight, and Grant could see she must have been defending a group of children huddled between the wall and buttress of the bridge. Jafri kept the group of children in sight, watching their faces as he drove the tip of the dagger into the woman's back. She shuddered and gasped, her legs shook and as he pulled the blade back out, she relaxed and lay still.

Grant barrelled into Jafri at an astonishing closing speed and took the man to the ground. Jafri was winded for a moment, but suddenly started lashing out with the blade in his left hand. He had dropped the other blade onto the pavement with a clatter. Grant felt the slash against his shoulder, felt the knock of the blade upon bone. It did not hurt, but he knew that he had been wounded. Jafri was getting to his feet and reaching for the other dagger. Grant rolled to put some distance between them, kept glancing behind him to keep Jafri in his vision. He could feel the slash now. It burned and froze all at once. Jafri was back on his feet and breathing heavily. Grant stepped off to the side. He unbuckled his leather belt and ripped it out of the belt loops. He held onto the buckle like a knuckle duster and wrapped the belt once around his hand. Jafri smirked and came in for his attack, but Grant was quick and flicked the tip of the belt into the man's face like a wet towel in a men's changing room full of high jinks. The leather cracked in Jafri's face, and he yelped and recoiled. Grant advanced and flicked twice more, catching the man both times in the face. Jafri shook his head and lunged with the blade in his left hand. Grant kept his eyes on both blades and swung the belt around Jafri's left hand. He kicked out and caught him in the kneecap. Jafri swung the other blade like a great pendulum and Grant stepped back. He could hear the swish of the blade through the air. He was no longer aware of ambient noise around him, of the screams, the sobbing, the sirens or anything else. For now, it was this moment and nothing else. The belt had become tangled with the blade and Grant whipped it to one side. The knife clattered onto the pavement and slid into the road, but it had slashed the belt and snagged, and the belt shot out of Grant's hand. Jafri said nothing, but he had noticed that his quarry was now unarmed. He lunged forwards and Grant kicked the blade aside. He looked at the group of terrified children behind Jafri. There was six or seven feet between them. More than enough room to duck out from behind the buttress.

"Run!" he shouted. "Now!"

They did, or most of them did, and Jafri turned around. Grant charged forwards, just two feet away when Jafri turned and swung back with the knife. Grant felt the blade go in. He caught hold of Jafri's wrist and the Pakistani tried to wrench the knife back but was no match for Grant's strength.

Strangely, it did not hurt. But Grant felt the unnatural presence of the blade, his body aware that it should not have been there. He felt his heart rate go crazily fast, his heart pounding and the blood surging through his veins and arteries. His brain seemed to send out signals too. He knew he had been stabbed, but the brain was reminding him of it constantly. He could feel nausea washing through him. Knew he did not have much time.

Grant could see his daughter, Chloe. Memories of happy events, snapshots of pictures he had taken. A time before the drink had driven his family away. A time he had wasted and squandered and in his last moments on this earth, a time he regretted losing. He glanced at the two terrified girls from the group; still huddled against the buttress. He was no longer thinking. He was well past that stage now.

It was a series of subconscious reasoning – action and reaction. Like knocking a cup from the draining board and putting your toe out to break its fall. You never thought to do it, it was merely reactionary instinct. All that he could process, was that if he died now, if he dropped and fell, those girls would be Jafri's next victims. He was already pushing Jafri backwards. Backwards towards the railings of the viewing point cut into the walls of the bridge. He mustered more strength, more momentum. He kept the man's wrist clamped tight, the blade sheathed within his own body, and powered down through his core, through his strong legs for the final push and slammed Jafri's back into the iron railings.

Chapter Three

"I don't get it," Mary snapped indignantly.

"I'm sorry," Grant said, replacing the binoculars to the top of the bookcase. He closed the glass doors and drew the curtains. He nodded towards the light switch. "It's okay, turn the lights back on now."

"Turn them on yourself," she said, walking out of the room. Grant noticed her bare shoulders, the low-cut dress showing them off, along with a tiny dolphin tattoo on her right shoulder. It added an air of mystery to her, and he wondered if there were any more and where they might be. She flicked on the kitchen light and dropped the takeaway bags on the table, next to a four-pack of Heineken and a bottle of chardonnay. She had everything planned. In the light of the kitchen the low-cut dress looked like part of the plan as well.

"Look, I just..."

"Don't think you can snap at me like that, Grant. I've put up with enough shit in my life, I'm not making the same mistakes again." She placed her hands on her hips, cocked her head defiantly and stared at him. "What the hell were you looking at out there anyway? It's almost dark outside."

"I was watching a boat."

"A boat?" She looked at him like he was crazy. "In the bloody dark, this far up the creek?"

"Yes."

"Probably poachers. You 'seen the deer over there?" her accent slipped a little towards the Cornish end of the scale. "There's stock fencing and a gated entrance to the estate. Much easier to drag a deer carcass down through the woods and into a boat."

"That goes on?"

She shrugged. "It all goes on down here." Her eyes flared for a moment. "No reason to shout at me like you did... I've put up with enough shit in my life, I'll not put up with any more."

"Okay," he said quietly, not sure what she had meant, but certain he would be told in time. He stepped closer and placed both hands on her shoulders. It was the first time he had touched her. Her skin was soft and smooth. "It was nice of you to come round."

"You invited me!"

"I did?"

"Yes. The other night. You said it would be nice to just get a takeaway, have a quiet night in."

Grant cursed inwardly. He had said that was what he planned to do, rather than going to local pub again, where he had taken most of his meals since arriving. Mary worked there as a part-time barmaid. He had enjoyed her company, enough to go on the date in Truro. However, when she floated the idea of getting together again, he realised that he couldn't miss the second scheduled time and date that Commander Maitland had made for him. He noted, for the thousandth time, that he really was shit socially. Or maybe he was just out of practice?

He looked at her, all red hair and fire in her eyes. She was attractive, but damaged. He could tell that much. But he could tell as much when he looked in the mirror. She was keen on him, that much was true. And women hadn't been beating down his door for the past couple of years. Not since his divorce. Not even before. He studied her eyes. Hazel, glossy. She had an honest face. He could tell being in her company wouldn't be an easy ride. But where was the fun in that? She looked back at him, her expression a little softer now. There was a comfortable height advantage on his part, and she tilted her head upwards. Her lips were soft and pouted a little. He took it as a sign and leaned in to kiss her. She kissed him back and he relaxed, it wasn't often he read the signs right, but he was about due. She kissed softly, and he matched her. He'd learned early on to step up the pace or tone it down accordingly, but whatever you did, match her mood and take your cues. He'd also learned that if you didn't rush this part, you got far more of her later.

She pulled away and smiled, her expression was one of contentment. "Now that's more like it," she said. Grant leaned in again but managed to kiss fresh air as she turned around and opened one of the takeaway bags on the table. "I got you barbecued ribs. Most men like ribs. Or you can share my sweet and sour king prawns, whatever, I'm easy..." She turned around. "Well, not easy! I mean..."

Grant regained some composure, managed to put his lips and tongue away in time. "Ribs will be great!" he said, a little too enthusiastically. He was ebbing, the blood pounding through him a little less. So much for his tried and tested strategies.

"I got noodles and rice as well," Mary said as she went

off in search of plates and cutlery. Grant wished her luck, he hadn't used them yet, didn't know where to find them. She bent down and opened a cupboard door. Her backside was shapely in the snug-fitting dress. She seemed to realise this, and dropped down, squatting somewhat elegantly on her heels. She came back up with two plates and put them down beside the food. She smiled at him, a little coyly. Grant couldn't tell if it was an act or a ploy, but he knew he hadn't wanted anybody more in years. She was good, because she all but had him in her hand. "And wantons."

"Great," he said dumbly.

He thought he'd better be pro-active and set about in search of cutlery rather than just stare at her figure. He'd found the coffee mugs and he had learned how to use the somewhat complicated espresso machine. It probably cost more than his car, which admittedly had seen better days, but still. He drank his coffee black and unsweetened, and he needed it like an engine needed fuel. He rarely ate breakfast, often skipped lunch and pub had provided him with pies and steaks and fish and chips for most of the week so he hadn't bothered to search for the cutlery or plates. He soon found the correct drawer and took out two spoons and two forks. Mary took a spoon from him and set about dishing out the food. She was taking control more than Grant liked, but he hadn't kissed like that in a long time and if he thought about it the kiss had been about the best he'd ever had. Mary's lips were soft and wet like sliced strawberries and her tongue had been so soft and gentle, probing tentatively. There was a freshness and tenderness he couldn't remember feeling before. One kiss and he was falling hard.

Mary smiled over her shoulder as she led the way into

the lounge. "Got any music?" she asked, kicking off her shoes and coiling herself up on the sofa like a cat.

Grant didn't know. He doubted Maitland's taste in music or his wife's for that matter would appeal to the thirty-year-old in front of him. "I'm not sure," he said. In truth, he was hungry now and just wanted to eat.

She shrugged. "So how come you're staying here?"

The question had come as he had bitten into the rib. He chewed, felt sauce on the corner of his mouth. She smiled and leaned forward, wiped the sauce from his cheek with the tip of her finger. She tasted it, then popped a king prawn into her mouth. Grant didn't know if he was more turned on, or whether it turned his stomach. A little of both, perhaps.

"It's my boss's home. Or second home," he said. "He's from money and so is his wife, so I think he has homes all over the place."

"So why are you here?"

"I'm divorced. I live in a little apartment near Camden Lock. My boss thought I'd do better down here," he said. "For my recovery."

"Recovery?"

"I was injured. Stabbed."

"Oh god!" she exclaimed. "Seriously?"

"Yes."

"No," she sighed. "I meant, were you seriously stabbed?"

"I suppose so," Grant replied. "It's hard to imagine a stabbing that isn't serious."

"Where?" she asked, licking sweet and sour sauce from her lips.

"In London..."

"Oh, for god's sake!" she laughed. "I meant, where on your body?" She shook her head and smiled.

Grant smiled too. He hadn't meant to take her questions so literally, but it was funny now. "In my stomach," he replied. "And a gash on my shoulder. It was bad. And I needed a bit of work inside my stomach to get it all stitched back together. I had to eat scrambled eggs for the first three weeks. I'm not sure the surgeon would approve of my meals at the pub."

"Can I see it?"

The question came out of the blue, he hadn't expected it. He hadn't shown anybody else either. Only the medical staff, his own doctor for follow-up appointments and his police federation representative. There was a compensation case in process. He doubted he'd be living in his tiny apartment for much longer. He had been told to get the best deal he should take six-months leave on grounds of mental anguish. He couldn't have begun to contemplate that. He was champing at the bit to get back to work as it was. And he wasn't one to play the system or screw it all together. Procedures and human rights, yes. Fake depression, no. In truth he felt pretty good. The wound no longer hurt now that the external stitches and staples had been removed. The internal ones would dissolve soon, if they hadn't already and the wound to his shoulder had been relatively quick to heal. Considering what happened, there were plenty who encouraged him to remain on sick leave, but he had had enough of it already. If it wasn't for Maitland's assignment on the side, he would have asked to go back to work last week.

"I was hoping you'd see it, but not like this," he grinned wolfishly.

"No way!" she laughed. "I'm not sleeping with you if it's all gross and stuff!"

He laughed but wasn't entirely sure how serious she had been. He put his plate down on the coffee table and wriggled forward to the edge of the sofa. He lifted his shirt to his rib cage. Mary took in his toned stomach, the remains of his six-pack, which had started to fade after so much time away from the gym located in the basement of his headquarters. He wasn't a serious gym goer, but he tended to go after his shifts, when others headed to the pub. It was easier to be out of the way of temptation, than to skirt the dangers of its periphery, and easier to have a credible excuse. Mary cocked her head when she saw the scar. It was jagged and approximately six inches long. She reached out slowly and touched it. Her fingernails were sharp, and he flinched a little. She removed her finger, kissed the tip and patted the scar again.

"That will pass. I won't kick you out of bed for that," she said. She leaned in and kissed him again. Softly, her lips open enough to be sensual, but closed enough to signal it was merely a kiss. She sat back in the sofa, tucked her legs underneath herself and picked up her plate. "Did it hurt?" she asked.

Grant picked up a rib and felt the fires below extinguish once more. He bit off a good mouthful and chewed. He'd almost finished it when he said, "At the time, no. I mean, I knew I'd been stabbed, but it didn't hurt. I felt it slowing me down, the effects of the injury. It stung later, and then hurt like hell until I got into the hospital." He realised he did not have a drink. Nor did Mary. "Do you want a drink?"

"Please."

"Wine?"

"Yes, please."

He got up and walked out to the kitchen, noticing a light that shone briefly past the window. He looked out through his own reflection in the glass, to the quiet road at the rear, or technically, the front of the house. There was a gravelled parking area, enough for three cars, where Grant had parked his old Alfa Romeo. The road beyond connected most of the villages and tiny hamlets on the point, but at this time of night there would only be the odd dog walker or car coming home. The light had looked like a torch. The glow of an orange streetlamp lit up a good proportion of the area. There was nobody out there now. He turned back to the table and unscrewed the wine. He's never been a wine drinker, had no issues pouring it into the glass he had taken out of an open display rack. He filled himself a large glass of water and returned to the lounge. He froze, the two glasses in his hands, the wine and water spilling out and onto the oak floor as he stopped abruptly in his tracks.

"Stand still," one of the men said. He was the man with the shotgun, so Grant did as he was told.

The other man was standing behind Mary, who was still holding her plate. He bent down and knocked it out of her hand, scattering rice, noodles and sauce all over the coffee table. She flinched and let out a little yelp. She was recoiling, almost hugging herself tightly.

Both men wore balaclavas and were both dressed in greasy jeans and work jackets. Grant noted the tattoos on the hands and wrists of the man brandishing the shotgun. He feared shotguns, had seen what one could do to an unfortunate security guard early on in his career. What he feared most was the lack of skill it took to use one with devastating effect. Grant felt dumb holding the drinks. He felt like downing the wine, even though he hated the taste of it.

Fifty-nine days...

"Put down those *bleddy* glasses and kneel on the floor," the man with the shotgun said in a heavy Cornish accent.

Grant weighed his odds. To someone holding a shotgun he was no threat at all. If they were going to kill him, then they would probably have done it by now. He watched Mary's expression, but it was one of sheer terror. "Do it!" the man barked. His Cornish accent was as thick as Grant had ever heard and the man raised the last word of each sentence at least an octave.

Grant stepped across to the dresser and put the two glasses down. He turned around and kneeled slowly. The man behind Mary stepped around the sofa and Grant could see he held a roll of duct tape. His heart raced, but the barrels of the side-by-side shotgun were menacing and unwavering. The unarmed man was soon behind Grant, and he grabbed his arms roughly. Grant did not make it easy for him, keeping his arms locked. The man struggled but was strong and he pulled backwards against the joints and Grant gave. He wrapped the tape tightly, round his wrists several times. Then he ripped the tape and stood back, pleased with his handiwork. Without warning he kicked Grant in the face, and he recoiled backwards into the dresser. The man kicked again and again. Grant heard Mary scream, followed by the man with the shotgun shouting at her to shut up.

"Here, take this," the other man said, holding the shotgun out for his companion. "I want a go." He paced over and the other man took the weapon. He got closer to Grant and swung down a savage punch into his face. Grant felt his teeth crack together. He could feel a chip of tooth somewhere in his mouth. He clenched his teeth tightly as the man rained a series of blows down on him.

Grant's ears were ringing, and his eyes were clouded and wet. He was dizzy, and his face felt thick and numb. The other man was laughing. The two had forgotten about Mary, and she looked as if she was about to move off the sofa when the man now holding the shotgun turned around.

"Where do you think you're off to?" She froze and he walked over to her. He held the shotgun in his right hand grabbed her right breast with his spare hand and gave it a squeeze. "Bugger me, that's got to be nearly three-pound in weight!" She recoiled away and the man laughed. He turned around and shouted to his companion, who was taking a breather from pummelling Grant around the head. "I'm going to give her one, if it's alright with you?" he said. Grant noted that he was better spoken than the tattooed man, little accent and he did not round off his words.

"No!" Mary shouted.

"Shut up!" the man snapped, spinning around and grabbing her by the wrists. He dragged her off the sofa and she kicked wildly. He pushed her away, then pulled her back with such force that she fell into him. He ducked low and had her over his shoulder with as much well-practised precision as a coalman unloading a fifty-kilo sack. He walked past Grant and handed the shotgun over to the other man and made his way into the kitchen.

Grant tried to stand, but the man kicked him back down, and without his hands to balance or break his fall, he fell into the dresser and cracked his head. The man followed it up with several savage punches, and Grant could feel his consciousness tested. He tried to focus. The man grabbed him by the throat and bent down, staring at him. Grant could see his eyes behind the torn holes in the woollen mask. He noticed the colour of one of the man's eyes had bled into the white. He was reminded of the missing Madeleine McCann's distinctive iris. The man's eyes were dark brown. He drew closer, cigarette smoke on his clothes, a sharp aroma on his breath, enough to make Grant want to gag.

"You hear me?" he said quietly. Grant nodded. He could hardly breathe. He tried to splay his arms, but the bindings were too strong. He nodded again. "Good. Get *yer* arse back in that fancy Italian car and get back to the smoke where *he* belong..." He gave Grant's throat a shake. "You hear *us*?" Grant nodded. The man pushed him down onto the ground. Grant grunted and looked up, just in time to see the sole of the man's work boot coming down towards his face. That was the last he remembered.

Chapter Four

"And you left the door unlocked?"

"Shouldn't be a crime."

"It's not."

"Then why does it matter?" Grant stared at the man in front of him, glanced across at the young female detective sitting next to him.

"They didn't break in."

"They weren't invited. And they had a gun." He pressed the icepack to his jaw, his eyes – everywhere, really. "That's a serious offence."

"Just ascertaining the situation."

"Ascertain all you like, but they entered the property, pointed a gun at us, beat the living shit out of me after tying me up and took my friend away saying they were going to rape her."

"You said…" The detective flicked through his notes, "*Give her one.* You never said, rape…"

The female detective looked across at her superior ranking officer not hiding the look of contempt. She turned back to Grant, her face impassive.

"Well in the context of taking her by force, and dragging her kicking and screaming, I would say it was safe to assume that *giving her one*, meant rape." Grant sipped the coffee the young female detective had made him earlier and shook his head. "Look, detective...?"

"Detective *Chief* Inspector Warleggan..."

"DCI Warleggan, I'm a police officer myself..."

"I know."

"You do?"

"Of course. This is Cornwall."

"That small, eh?"

"Well connected, that's all."

"My friend..."

"Is safe and well."

"She is?"

"Yes. And she doesn't want to press charges."

"What?" Grant looked at the female detective. "You buy that? Sorry, what is your name?"

"Detective Sergeant Clark."

"Do you think that is acceptable, DS Clark?"

"No, it's not."

"Thank you, DS Clark!" DCI Warleggan said sharply. He looked back at Grant. "If she doesn't want to press charges..."

"She doesn't have a choice!"

"She might."

"She was abducted! We were threatened at gun point! I was tied and beaten! She can't pick and choose over offences like that," Grant said.

"She's safe and well. She made the call."

Grant alternated the coffee for the icepack and pressed it against his swollen eye. It hurt like hell. "Where is she?"

"I said she was safe and well."

"Do you think she knew the attackers?"

"No. Why?"

"Because I can't think of any other reason for not wanting to take this further," Grant said, taking the icepack away from his eye socket and cheek. "What happened after she was taken? She called you."

The detective leaned back in the chair. He looked comfortable, unhurried. "Why are you down here?"

"Recuperation, a free holiday," answered Grant. "And *I* asked you a question first. What happened after she was taken?"

"You're familiar with the chain of command, are you not, DI Grant?" Warleggan asked. "I understand you were a DCI once. A long time, and more than a few mistakes ago."

Grant shrugged. "Public record," he said. "Even *you* could look it up."

"Well, I did."

"And what did it say?"

"That you falsified evidence."

DS Clark looked between the two men. She seemed to be enjoying the cock fight. Grant didn't think she liked her boss much, his comments about rape had shown as much. "What's your biggest case to date, DCI Warleggan? Did it involve cows on the road, or a stolen bicycle? Mine was spending four months of my life undercover with right wing extremists. My last case had me chasing down an Islamic terrorist."

"We *do* get the news down here, DI Grant," he said nonchalantly. "How's the stab wound?" He glanced at DS Clark. "We have a big city celebrity in our midst. I'm surprised he's not signed up to go into the jungle with all the other celebrities nobody has ever heard of."

"I think they film in the autumn, Sir," DS Clark said amiably.

Warleggan scowled at her, closed his notebook. "Well, I think we've got all we need."

"Where is Mary?"

"She's safe. If you don't know where she lives, I certainly won't tell you."

Grant shook his head. "What station do you work out of?"

"Why?"

"So, I can call and find out what progress you're making."

"I'll get a log number and you can call one-zero-one."

"You may want to re-think that, DCI Warleggan. I'm tired now, but tomorrow is another day. You may want to put your cock away and give me some professional courtesy. You may find your arse bounces off the fucking walls tomorrow and you rethink whether your career is in the Devon and Cornwall Police or walking around in a yellow high-visibility jacket doing security at the Boardmasters Festival. Tomorrow is the day you may just lose your pension," Grant said, his eyes boring into Warleggan's own. "Now, if you really *have* finished, fuck off out of my house and don't let the door hit your fat arse on your way out."

Chapter Five

The sun was bright, and it shone through the window at the eastern side of the house. The lounge windows faced south, and the sun remained on the house all through the day, with the sun setting over the headland at the highest end of the creek. Grant finally realised why 'south facing' was always a popular phrase touted on property programmes. It really was a feature worth having. He thought about his apartment in Camden Lock. He got the sun for about forty-five minutes a day in the summer months. He couldn't ever recall having seen it from his apartment in the winter. But then, he was hardly ever in. He picked up the post, dropped his head on the pillow most nights for a few hours. His satellite TV had been playing up for a few months now, but he'd never got around to having it fixed. There was little point.

He drank his third cup of black coffee, watched the water subside from the creek. He figured it had been high again at around six-am. It was now eight. The big black and white bird was still dipping for shrimp or whatever it was it was searching for. He looked back at the photocopies of newspaper clippings, the police reports, pathology reports and printouts of internet-based news reports. He had a pattern. And it made him feel uneasy. Singularly, the information was merely a collection of facts and dates. It was the skill of the investigator to create a pattern, use relative assumption and deduct meaning.

The first story was a sad tale, but one told so many times in recent years. The Syrian refugee crisis had become apathetic. So many news features had desensitised the public to their plight. Naturally, there were charities and organisations helping the refugees no end, and the governments of the countries of western Europe had all taken in refugees, some more than others, and given aid to the camps. But it had been news for so long, that it was dropping from the front pages of the papers and the lead features of the programmes, and in some cases, dropped from the schedule altogether. The crisis had peaked with the tragic images of a three-year-old boy. Those images had been the reason Germany had made the short call to allow a million refugees in practically overnight. Alan Kurdi was the little boy whose body was photographed drowned and being removed from the beach near the fashionable Turkish town of Bodrum. It was front page news, and TV news lead story for a week. Celebrities were outraged and talking about nothing else. Some were even going to sing songs. Appeals were made. Slowly, the crisis faded from the news, with one or two pieces a week flashing across the screens of the world. Then Brexit came along, and Donald Trump and rockets launched high above North Korea and the world looked inwards for a while, contemplating the insanity on their own doorsteps. War in Syria rolled on, family lines were wiped off the face of the earth. Russia continued to back the Syrian government, the rest of the world complained, but failed to step up and stand up for fear of waking the giant sleeping Russian bear, and refugees continued to migrate to Europe, after outrageous rights such as protection, safety and survival. Trump's fall, Biden's rise, the Covid pandemic, the invasion of Ukraine by Russia and a series of UK prime ministers and financial crisis and the refugee migrant crisis became the norm and people no longer seemed to care because the news corporations had moved on.

Five people changed all of that. For a while, Cornwall had its very own Bodrum. The bodies of the Hafeez family were found on beaches and rocky sections of coastline from Maenporth to The Manacles, a notoriously dangerous section of reef on The Lizard. Qasim was forty-five-years-old, a doctor and back in his hometown of Aleppo, he ran a successful practice, drove a Mercedes and had coached football to under eleven-year-old boys. But that was before the war broke out. During the war he had operated on and treated casualties, unpaid, in a city hospital. He moved around a lot, because Syrian government forces and Russian pilots targeted the hospitals. He was an expert in his field as a paediatrician and had studied medicine in both Britain and France. He had even been educated at Oxford for a year on an exchange program. His wife, Yara was also a doctor, who had trained in France. She was forty-one but had taken a career break to bring up their four girls. Shabnam and Amira were twins aged 19, Fatma was seventeen and Gita was aged just fifteen. Yara never did manage to get her career back on track because of the war, but she assisted her husband in theatre when she could.

It was a tragic story, but one the West was becoming increasingly used to. A family drowned while seeking asylum. The remains of a torn rubber dingy was found on The Manacles. No possessions had been recovered. The bodies had no identification on them, but photo-fits and artist's impressions were made and distributed, largely on social media, and because of Qasim's humanitarian work in Syria, he was soon identified. No arrangements were made to collect the bodies. They had no family in the UK, and no family left alive in Syria. A tragic end to a family who had lived and witnessed more than anybody should. And with the Hafeez's, an entire family line had ended.

Grant read the reports from a variety of newspapers. The journalism varied in both approach and quality and the local press carried the story on for a while. It was a weekly paper and Grant saw five pieces in all. Nothing new appeared in any of the articles. The last story sparked mentions from the national papers. Cornwall had over-whelmingly voted out of Europe in the referendum, dubbed Brexit. It hadn't done the Duchy much good, the entire county was seen as small-minded and racist, as much of the south of England had voted to remain. The article mentioned the excessive price of Cornish homes, the high percentage of second homes and holiday lets, the lower-than-average wages and general employment challenges faced by the Cornish. In truth, Brexit was a cry for help with the British government. The Cornish felt margin-alised, despite good funding from the EU. Grant read with interest, considering the fact that he sat in the garden of a second home, in a village that was left three-quarters empty during the winter months. The locals worried if their pub would last with such a drop in winter trade. A real problem for villages all over the county. Cornwall had its problems, and all the papers enjoyed a good racist story. Good people had inevitably stepped up in time and raised both funds and awareness, that this Muslim family would suffer great indignity if they were cremated. Burial was the only method acceptable, and people from the Muslim community came forward with the finances, and arrangements were made for worshipers from a local Mosque to wash and wrap the bodies in an Islamic burial ceremony and a family burial site was secured at the council-run graveyard at Swanvale in the coastal town of Falmouth. It was to most people's horror that the grave was later vandalised. Small-minded racially driven actions by people in a county that had voted out of Europe. Brexit had been hijacked by remain voters who pointed a racist finger at anyone who wanted to change the status quo with Europe. The people who wanted a halt to immigration, to secure the country's borders had spoken. Cornwall never saw immigration, other than Polish workers who came to pick and harvest what would have ruined in the ground if it had been left to local workers. What Cornwall wanted was recognition from the country's government and a halt to fishing quotas, as well as more freedoms within agriculture. Nevertheless, the county was seen as a last bastion for the small-minded and now the national papers had their racism articles written and published. From a news angle, it could not have gone better.

Grant put down a piece by The Daily Mail. It was as sensational as it had been possible to write. He rubbed his eyes gently. The bruising had come out overnight. He looked a sight. His face was swollen, his right eye puffed shut and he had a split on his top lip. He had chipped a tooth at the back, and it felt sharp and rough when he probed it with his tongue. Which was all the time, now that he knew it was there. He drank more coffee, stared out across the ebbing expanse of water. The thought of that poor family, desperate enough to embark on such a dangerous journey, so close at the end. So near, yet so far. They must have been terrified. He looked back at the police and coastguard reports. He made a few notes. He had questions that needed answering. The reports were too light in his opinion. Conveniently so.

Chapter Six

Grant drove the Alfa Romeo through Point Loe, the burble of the exhaust note echoing off the houses as he briefly travelled parallel with the creek. He wondered if the noise had anything to do with the empty houses. The Creekside houses were large and constructed primarily of glass, chrome and seasoned wood. All hard surfaces and with little in the way of furnishings inside, or open windows to absorb the sound. Like when you viewed an empty house and it echoed in a way that it never did again when you came back and moved your belongings in after renting or buying it.

The road wound round to the left and past the pub. It was just past nine-thirty, and a woman was sweeping cigarette butts off the steps and out into the road. The smoking ban hadn't done much for the frontage of places like this. The last time Grant had been in the pub, three-quarters of the clientele had been sheltering from rain in the lee of the porch, as a squall had come up the creek from the sea, leaving Grant alone with Mary at the bar. That's when they had gelled, and he had agreed to her suggestion of a date. It troubled Grant that she had been so forward, and considering what had happened could it have been merely a coincidence, or had there been an element of gameplay?

He thought about Mary, needed to know what had happened. Had the men abused her? DCI Warleggan had said that she had not wanted to press charges, but with the events that had transpired, the offences carried out, that wasn't an option. The police would be obligated to investigate and seek criminal prosecution. Grant suspected that Mary had a complicated past. She had intimated that she had suffered enough, her reaction at him shouting for her to switch off the lights when he had spotted the man looking back at him with the binoculars from across the creek had seemed like a line drawn in the sand. She hadn't been out as much as she had made out, the long-time closure of the nightclub had shown that, and for an attractive thirty-year-old woman, there would have to be a reason for her lack of a social life. Perhaps it was the fact her friends had moved on with partners and had children, or even careers. Grant suspected she had a child herself and was a single mother. Nothing wrong in that. Pretty standard. However, Grant had given thought to the possibility that one of the men had been her lover, or ex-lover and had decided to warn him off with the help of a friend. Small town stuff. In that case, perhaps she had wanted to avoid further problems with an estranged partner, perhaps even her child's father. Maybe she had even reconciled and that was her reason for not wanting to take matters further. He was assuming a hell of a lot, but emotionally, he hadn't been in the best place last night. Sleep had completely evaded him, and thoughts always took on a complicated dimension in the early hours.

He slowed the car as he passed the pub. He did not recognise the woman cleaning the steps. He peered through the doorway as he slowed. Should he stop and go in? He thought not. The ex-partner scenario might make more problems for her. He needed to speak with Mary, but he knew he would need to be discreet. He floored the accelerator and powered past. The road widened and the village was left behind him as he headed towards the A39, the main Truro to Falmouth road. Grant had done some internet research on his laptop and found what he thought would be the station most likely for DCI Warleggan to be based. Cornwall's policing was a curious affair. Devon and Cornwall Constabulary policed the largest geographical area in the entire United Kingdom. It had to cope with an influx of eleven-million people each summer season, yet the force was shrinking, and severe cutbacks had been made. Nothing new there, but the force had closed its principal station in Truro, Cornwall's capital, and another in Falmouth. The constabulary's headquarters were ninety miles away in Exeter. Many of the stations were faceless facilities where the public could gain no access. A non-emergency telephone number was recommended and a 'we'll come to you' attitude had replaced an approachable policing presence within the community. Grant couldn't see any good from the approach, it served only to alienate people and leave them feeling cut-off from the law. From what he could ascertain, both Bodmin and Camborne stations seemed the only options from where DCI Warleggan and any CID presence could be maintained at any strength.

He chose Camborne as it was closer. The drive took him along a series of sweeping roads. They were narrow, tree-lined or walled in by stone hedges, and extremely fast-moving. Many of the drivers seemed to possess the gift of telepathy, crowning the centre of the road as they negotiated the corners. On several occasions he put the Alfa Romeo's paintwork into the uncut foliage sprouting from the hedges as oncoming vehicles clearly cut onto his side of the road. He was no steady driver, but he felt whisked along in places. He dropped his speed as he entered Lanner. There were digital signs flashing up the thirty-miles-per-hour speed limit, and the drivers at least slowed for these, then raced to the next one in time to hammer on their brakes. This wasn't the Cornwall he had expected. He could see that prosperity found its way into pockets of the county, but this wasn't one of them. There were council houses, new-builds and dilapidated cottages long since extended with block extensions far from keeping them in character. He crowned the hill and drove down into Redruth. He changed his mind about Lanner, but only just. Redruth was an experience and this coming from a man who had policed some of the most deprived parts of London. He missed the road he needed and ended up skirting around a one-way system to enjoy the sights. There were well-supported shops and buildings turned to flats, but within minutes he was driving through a tree-lined street with grand houses on either side. Huge affairs with gardens and parking. These would have been two or three-million-pound homes in parts of London. He doubted they were worth a quarter of that in this town. They looked old and Grant remembered reading somewhere that Redruth had been once been a prosperous town, one of the country's leading centres of industry when copper and tin were mined throughout the nineteenth century and within the richest three-square miles on earth at the height of the tin and copper industry. A right-hand turn and all this was quickly forgotten and he skirted an area of abject poverty once more. The next couple of miles were taken up with a long road of houses, industrial estates, retail parks, budget foreign supermarkets and a college. This stretch of built-up area was Pool and it connected Redruth with Camborne. When he entered Camborne, he changed his mind and re-evaluated Redruth a little more positively. The journey had become progressively more depressing. It was a far cry from The Point and the other places like Feock and Mylor he had driven through recently. Cornwall was a county of extremes. There appeared to be a large scale in both income and social divide. He doubted that these poorer areas were going to see some of the eleven-million extra people spending their money each summer.

Camborne Police Station was on his left, and he parked easily enough. He followed the signs to the main entrance. The building was constructed from granite with concrete and render extensions. There were traffic police vehicles parked in the lined bays and smaller community policing cars curbing an area of grass. Two uniformed officers exited and walked past him without looking at him. He thought his swollen eye and bruises warranted a second glance, but that was probably one of the reasons why he had made detective at just twenty-four.

The man running the desk was a standard-issue community support officer. He was late fifties, growing thickly around his middle and did not look up as Grant entered. Grant coughed. The man continued to tidy some paper and check his computer monitor. He started to type slowly.

"Grant," he said. "I'm here to see DCI Warleggan."

The man did not look up. "He's in a meeting."

"Go fetch him. Tell him to hurry."

The man looked up this time. "Who are you?"

"Today, I'm your boss. Now go fetch him, or your best bet would be to start typing up a new CV."

"Who the hell are you?" the man said, flushing red. His voice was wavering as he saw the intensity in Grant's eyes.

"Acting Detective Superintendent Grant, Special Branch," Grant said, then added, "Are you still here?"

The desk officer got up without further word and opened the glass door behind him. He was away from his desk for a few minutes, then came back in and nodded. "He's on his way," he said, his attitude doing a one-eighty. "Can I get you a coffee?"

"No, thanks," Grant said, then turned and looked at the walls. They were mainly of drug-related posters and domestic abuse. There was an anti-terrorism check list, but it was four years old. Grant had helped design the current poster.

Warleggan opened the door and stared at him. "Problem?" he asked incredulously.

"That depends."

"On what?"

"On whether you're in a better frame of mind," Grant said. "Find us an office where we can talk."

"For what?" Warleggan was fuming. "I said all I needed to last night."

Grant reached into his pocket and retrieved two well folded envelopes. He took one and handed it to him. Warleggan pulled out the letter and read. The duty officer was watching from behind the desk. Grant couldn't resist. In ten minutes, the whole station, and more likely the entire Cornish designation of officers would know. For the kick of it Grant recited the letter as Warleggan read. "To whom it may concern... After his recent promotion to that of Detective Chief Inspector, following recent events in the fight against terrorism and subsequent award and commendation for bravery... that was The George Cross, by the way..." Grant added. "The rank of Acting Detective Superintendent has been awarded to DCI Grant, transcending all of Her Majesty's Police Forces on the United Kingdom mainland and Commonwealth Territories..." Grant smiled as Warleggan lowered the letter. "To surmise, it goes on to say that every courtesy will be extended, and co-operation given... signed, the Home Secretary and The Chief Commissioner..."

Warleggan handed back the letter. "What is it you want?"

"Just your undivided time and co-operation. Are we A1 fucking clear on that?"

Chapter Seven

DCI Warleggan led Grant into the CID offices. There were two detectives, both male and late forties drinking coffee by a whiteboard. One was pushing the scales towards overweight a bit too much to run after criminals and the other had had a good go at growing a hipster beard, only it was grey in too many places. He had a lot of crumbs in it as well. He held half a Danish pastry in one hand and a cup of something hot in the other. There were photographs pinned to the edges of the whiteboard, a mind-map in the centre. A timeline had been jotted in the bottom right corner. They seemed to be sharing a joke rather than theories.

DS Clark came out of a side door studying a sheaf of papers. She looked up when she saw Grant and did a double take. She walked around the row of desks and stood by the two male detectives.

"Is this it?" Grant asked.

"What do you mean?" DCI Warleggan asked somewhat defensively.

"Your CID. Are there more officers?"

"Of course," he nodded. "We have six more out on enquiries into ongoing investigations. There are a dozen detectives stationed at Bodmin but they're all working on cases. And three are on annual leave."

"Who worked on the Hafeez deaths?"

"The what?"

"The Syrian family who were found drowned near Falmouth."

Warleggan frowned, then nodded. Realisation finally hitting home. "Why?"

"Because I asked you."

"Why are Special Branch concerned with this?" Warleggan scoffed. "And why have they sent down a tainted officer to poke about?"

"Tainted?" Grant felt himself flush. His heart raced. It usually did that before he punched someone in the face. Instead, he said, "Explain yourself, DCI Warleggan."

"You're a DCI, not a regular inspector, I get it. Big deal."

"You read the letter. It's Acting Detective Superintendent, actually."

"Let me see that letter again."

Grant handed him the envelope. Warleggan took it and read it once more. He handed it to DS Clark. "Get that photocopied, Lucy."

Grant swiped it back. She was reading it, her eyebrow raised. "No. Sorry, no copies permitted. Orders." He perched back against a desk. "I need a coffee."

Warleggan cocked a head towards DS Clark. "See to that, Lucy."

She made to move, but Grant caught her arm. He looked back at the two detectives standing by the white-board. "Everyone a DS here?"

The overweight man shook his head. "Detective Constable Hastings, Sir."

"Great. I'll have a black coffee, no sugar, thanks."

DS Clark smiled at Grant. She turned and placed the sheaf of papers on an empty desk behind her.

DCI Warleggan's face was flushing red with anger. He shrugged and nodded towards his office. "In here, if you please, *Acting* Superintendent Grant."

Grant walked into the office in front of him and moved behind the desk. He pulled out DCI Warleggan's leather swivel chair and sat down, beckoning the man to sit on the plain wooden chair. "I want to talk about the Hafeez family. I have read the reports, and it seems that the police report is vague. Downright shoddy, in fact."

Warleggan looked like he was about to implode. He pulled out the chair reserved for his own visitors and sat down heavily. There was a knock on the door and DC Hastings opened it holding Grant's cup of coffee. He stared at Grant behind his chief's desk, tried and failed to regain composure, act like it was no big deal, and placed the coffee in front of Grant. He walked back out and closed the door behind him. The office was designed with a large glass wall. Grant remembered when this had become the norm, it made cases of sexual harassment and bullying in the workplace as transparent as the window itself. Grant glanced to his right and saw all three detectives and two uniformed officers, who had just dropped in to see the show, looking directly at him. Warleggan side glanced too, he looked back at Grant, thoroughly humiliated. "Vague?" he said, his tone hostile.

"I believe I ended on shoddy," Grant corrected him.

"They drowned whilst illegally entering the country."

"You don't get many illegal immigrants down here," Grant mused.

"What? We're bloody awash with them!"

"Really?"

"Half the workers on the farms were bloody Polish!" He paused. "Well, before Brexit. Most have gone home now."

"So, they were perfectly legal, then."

"Immigrants!" Warleggan snarled. "Catering, factories, agriculture... You name the job and there was an immigrant in it..."

"And now businesses are closing because they can't get the staff," he replied. "And I'll remind you, DCI Warleggan, that you are referring to legal workers from an EU member country," Grant said calmly. He could see the man was boiling. "They were legal as you and I."

"Not now! It was the best thing ever to leave the European Union."

"I'm sure the polish will still be welcome. Considering the good they did filling the roles nobody wants."

"If you say so..."

"So, you're not keen on immigrants, illegal or otherwise..."

Warleggan stopped himself. He looked at Grant coldly, but his eyes were dark brown, so he just looked mad. Grant's own eyes were grey-blue, and he'd seen enough in life to take the shine out of them. He returned a narrow glare, glacier-cold and unwavering. Unsettling. Warleggan looked away first, as Grant knew he would. "Look, I get it. You're here with a fancy letter and a new promotion, but I've got to work here," he said. "There's nothing amiss with the reports on that family. They came over in a shitty little rubber boat and drowned when it either capsized or ripped."

Grant nodded. "Sad. A whole family, the last of their line, wiped out."

"But the case is closed."

"I'm not happy with the findings."

"*You're* not?"

"Why do you say it like that?"

"Well, you've been sent by someone else. You're staying in Mike Maitland's place at Loe Creek. Coincidence? I think not..."

"You know Mike?"

He snorted. "Of sorts. We were at Hendon together. He was fast-tracked before there even was such a programme."

"You were friends?"

"No."

"But you knew him?"

"I *remember* him."

Grant nodded. He couldn't honestly say whether he would have been friends with Maitland had the man not been his mentor and boss. There was always the barrier of seniority and respect. And the man had commanded a lot of respect. Much of what was claimed of his achievements was bullshit. But he had ridden that particular wave and created a legend within the police service. The commander of Special Branch, with his finger on the pulse of terrorism. The man who ran the department that backed up MI5's intelligence work with hard arrests. It hadn't hurt that towards the end of the Northern Ireland troubles, Maitland had picked up a wounded police officer's weapon and killed an IRA terrorist before he could detonate an IED at a packed tube station. That had secured his status, cleared his path for the top. A legend had been born.

"So, you think it was just a case of drowning?"

"Of course!"

"And the vandalism to their grave?"

Warleggan shrugged. "Muslim haters."

"There are other targets. Community centres and mosques. A family's grave is low even for narrow minded racists."

"Then Muslim *immigrant* haters."

"Tell me about the boat."

"The boat?"

Grant sipped the coffee. It can't have been too hot when it was made, so he drank it down in one tepid gulp. It was budget supermarket instant. Nothing to savour, but it didn't hurt to keep the man waiting. He placed the cup down on a letter that was on the desk. There was no signature on it yet, but it had been signed off in Warleggan's name. The cup made a wet ring. Grant lifted it up, placed it down again to make another. He looked up at Warleggan, enjoyed the colour of the man's cheeks. He knew he could be a bastard, and now Warleggan knew it too. "The boat. Tell me about it."

"It was a fucking rubber boat. It ripped or capsized. They drowned. What more do you want?"

"It must have been quite a journey. I'm assuming they came in from France, but it's not the English Channel. This is the mouth of the Atlantic. Hundreds of miles in a rubber rowing boat?"

"They were desperate."

Grant shrugged. "I'm sure they were. No doubt about it."

"So?"

"So, a guy in his mid-forties and a woman knocking forty rowed over from France after walking across Europe from Syria with their four daughters, all of them under twenty years of age?"

"Perhaps all that walking got them fit?"

Grant stared at him. Warleggan already knew he wouldn't win staring back, so he glanced at his team, who were still looking at the show, and did not even try to busy themselves when he looked at them. "There are two facts here. As sure as day leads to night. One, is that you're a prick. Not a hard, useful prick, but more of a short, thin, flaccid prick of no particular use to anyone. In fact, you're not even a prick. You're a cunt." Grant leaned back in the swivel chair, put his hands behind his head. "The second fact is that the boat did not come over from France. I looked it up. It was a make and model produced in a town called Kuwuwing in the Yunan Provence of China. It wasn't a *bad* boat, a quarter the price of American and European offerings of the same specification, but not the sort of boat you use as a tender to your Four Winds, Bayliner or Regal on the weekends. Not what you want to be seen in at the yacht club. This was the sort of boat a well-meaning dad buys on a whim and comes back to the wrath of his more level-headed wife. It doesn't look as good, but it's a bit of family fun for a week or two's wages. It even has a small outboard. I reckon that would be a necessity on a crossing like that. You couldn't hope to row the channel, let alone a crossing all the way to Cornwall. The company made this model as a package with an engine, two-piece oars, a fuel tank and four lifejackets. So, you can't buy the boat on its own. Other than dads wanting to terrify their families and with their lack of seamanship knowledge, these boats suit cash-strapped fishermen. They don't care what the label on the boat says, or that it looks ten-years-old fresh out of the box..."

"I take it this is going somewhere?"

Grant nodded. "See what happens when you interrupt me again. I dare you," he leaned forwards and placed his hands on the desk, elbowed the ruined letter and a stapler out of the way. He watched Warleggan's eyes for a flicker. It was important to watch now, because if he didn't, then he wouldn't get his answer. "There was no equipment found along with the Hafeez family's bodies. No lifejackets, no fuel tank, no oars and no outboard." He reached into his jacket pocket and took out another envelope. He pulled out a series of photographs and dropped them in front of the detective. Warleggan picked them up and studied them one by one. "Although from the photographs you can clearly see from the scuff marks on the plastic transom that an outboard has been attached at some point." He held up a hand to silence the man before he spoke. "Now, I know you're going to say it might have come off and sunk. I mean, the sea here is rough most of the time, isn't it?" He watched Warleggan as the man nodded. "Except that the sea conditions were like a millpond. Not even a shore break. As you well know," he paused. "The second fact, apart from you being a certain derogatory description of a woman's genitalia, is that this boat was never sold in France. Nor was it sold in the rest of Europe. No, after its sale throughout Asia and the US, and its subsequent discontinuation, this boat was only ever sold in Britain as the entire package. I suppose they made the package up, got rid of all the extras they manufactured and moved on to making dildos or toilet brushes or parachutes, or whatever niche they could find and undercut. So, this package makes its way to Britain only. And guess where in particular? No, don't answer that. I dared you after all. You will not interrupt me again. No, this boat was destined to be sold all over the UK, but down here, in darkest Cornwall, one local merchant brought the entire shipment. The boat and package have been discontinued and one supplier, a large independent hardware and maritime depot not three miles from here bought the lot. Now how's that for research?" He leaned forwards and glared at him as he whispered, "That's what we call *detective* work."

DCI Warleggan looked at him, then broke away.

Grant had his answer.

Chapter Eight

"So, you were promoted to super for this assignment?" she asked.

"Acting super, yes," Grant threaded the Alfa Romeo through the traffic and paused as they passed a McDonalds. He was hungry and hesitated a moment before driving on. He was trying to eat well. Five years of drinking and a few falls off the wagon since he had taken his life back, but his liver still looked like lightly fried Foie Gras. He had been told by his doctor that the damage was entirely reversible. Prior to the incident at Westminster Bridge and his subsequent break in sobriety, he had been hitting the gym and the pool and eating well. He owed himself something better than a Big Mac and a vanilla shake.

"But what is the anti-terrorism angle?" DS Clark asked.

Grant changed gear, looking at her legs as he drove. She wore a pair of tight jeans, dark and smart. A white figure-hugging blouse, her coat draped across her lap. He had requested, or rather demanded she assist him with his inquiries. He needed local knowledge, and he had a feeling she did not like DCI Warleggan after his interview with them last night at the Hemingway House. He thought he might have found an ally. He also thought it may just piss Warleggan off a little more to lose his assistant as well as an entire loss of face in front of his men.

"There doesn't have to be an angle. My boss was concerned with some details. How he came across this is irrelevant. He was in a position to pull some rank, that's all."

She nodded. Grant glanced at her, and she smiled. "So, this letter you have, it pretty much gives you carte blanche?"

Grant hesitated before nodding. "Pretty much."

"Well, it certainly rattled the DCI."

"That was my intention. I suppose I went a bit far really. He's just racist, sexist and a bigot underneath, I don't like that. He shouldn't be in the job."

"He speaks highly of you too."

"I suppose he must."

"He said you falsified evidence and the guy got off because of it. He said you let down your team and your name was mud."

Grant shrugged like it did not matter. But it did. It had become everything and had cost him everything. His rank, his wife and family. The catalyst for so many ruined things, killed-off hopes and dreams. It had been the point to break his sobriety. After two years without alcohol, the failure of the case had left him falling off the wagon and yo-yoing between excess and abstinence. His wife had filed for divorce. He couldn't blame her. He had trouble looking in the mirror sometimes. He owed her some happiness, even if it was his absence that would give her that. "I didn't falsify anything," he said, measuredly.

"Hey, I don't need to know," she said.

"Yes, you do," Grant corrected her. "You're working with me, so I *want* you to know."

"Okay," she said, but he could tell she wasn't particularly bothered.

"We had all the evidence we needed. But there were a few things we couldn't dot and cross, so I left them out. We had more than enough for a successful prosecution and some serious prison time." Grant hit the brakes hard as the car in front misjudged a mini roundabout. "His defence was a young, hot-shot lawyer making a name for himself. He didn't just pull at the threads of what we, or rather *I*, omitted, he focused on it and virtually nothing else and by the end of the trial he had put so much doubt in the jury's mind, it could only really have gone one way."

"They're good at that," she nodded. "That was a factor of law that I didn't like. Defence lawyers are the worst, I don't know how they sleep at night."

"You and a lawyer traded blows on a case, right?"

She nodded. "He screwed me in the courtroom," she laughed. "He was my boyfriend. I wasn't letting him screw me in *any* room after that," she grinned. "A first-class lying bastard. I see the guy he defended sometimes. He's walking around free while his victim is too scared to go out. He's a rapist and my ex knows it."

Grant nodded. "That's why I don't like lawyers." He smiled. "But they're not as bad as your boss."

"No?"

"No. He's a lazy cop. Nothing worse than that. The police are the line between the public and their liberty. When their rights, liberty and welfare are threatened, the police need to do everything in their powers to serve and protect. DCI Warleggan has no love for outsiders or foreigners. Especially immigrants and asylum seekers. His bigotry and xenophobia have cost a family justice."

"He's like a lot of older police down here. They're gradually getting phased out, retired. It's getting better, but there are pockets of the police service where time hasn't caught up. I go to Exeter or Plymouth on a course and it's fine. Just like going back to Hendon for fast-track evaluation. Down in some of the places in Cornwall, the smaller towns and communities, and it's lost in the past. Some of the old coppers are dinosaurs. They're guarded and play the game, but after a few drinks and their guard comes down and they loosen up. They're old school. Like they're stuck in the seventies. Sexist, racist and homophobic and would still call a black man a *nignog* or *darkie* and a gay man a *poofter* if they had half the chance."

"I take it you're not from around here?"

"No. Hampshire. I moved down here when I finished uni."

"Usually the other way around, isn't it? You live here, go away to university, then have to live away to work off the debts and get a career."

She nodded. "I was lucky, a job came up and I moved. We holidayed here as a family at least twice a year. I sort of felt I grew up here. My father is Cornish, and we had his side of the family living down here. Cousins, aunts and my grandad. I had my fondest memories here. I got a job down here with the CPS. I was a lawyer."

"A lawyer!" Grant couldn't help himself. "Sorry," he said, then added, "I'm just not too fond of lawyers."

"Nor am I," she smiled. "To tell you the truth, I wasn't very good. I certainly wasn't a natural. I was dating a lawyer who was super good. And he showed that when he took me apart in the trial. When we split up, I just found myself wanting something completely different. I didn't last with the CPS and couldn't see myself doing property conveyancing and probate for the rest of my working life. I applied for Devon and Cornwall and got in. My law degree got me fast tracked and I made sergeant not long after my probationary period. I like what I do, and I like it more now I'm with CID," she paused. "We're here now. Just another fifty-metres on the right."

Grant nodded and turned into the site. It was a compound really, with two units on the one site. He could see access to a massive storage yard gated and fenced between the two buildings. He could see one marked tools and hardware and the other marked as marine goods, camping equipment and clothing. There were plenty of spaces and he parked the Alfa as far away from the other cars as possible. DS Clark opened her door and got out. Grant glanced at her rear as she pushed herself up. He hadn't intended to but was pleased he had. She was attractive and had a good figure. She had a comfortable demeanour as well, and he had talked easily with her. He was glad he had chosen her to work with over the overweight detective, or the one with half a Danish pastry in his beard.

They walked in through the automatic doors and DS Clark hovered around the counter, but Grant walked on past and down one of the cluttered aisles. She looked unsure for a moment, then followed him.

"What are you doing?" she asked, frowning at him.

"I like to get a feel for a place first," he said. "Take it all in a bit." He carried on walking, perusing some of the shelves, then stopped when he entered an area with marine and maritime equipment and clothing. He could see two boats and a small selection of canoes. They were open types and as he drew near, he noticed that these were inflatable models as well. He tapped the hull of one of them, surprised at how sturdy and rigid it was.

"We're here to look at the boat," she chided, nudging past him and standing in front of the yellow inflatable. "Not kayaks."

The boat was fitted with a three-horsepower petrol outboard with a manufacturer Grant did not recognise and slotted into the straps on the sides were a set of oars. Four lifejackets lay in the hull.

"A real beauty isn't she?" said a middle-aged man walking up behind them. He was wearing a sweatshirt with the store's logo on it. He banged a fist on the rubber hull and smiled. He didn't have many teeth in his smile, but that hadn't put him off trying. "I bought one of these beauties myself. All this for just six-hundred quid. You can't even buy a new outboard for that." He shrugged. "Alright, it's not an Evinrude or a Suzuki, but a lot of these factories all make the same stuff, just without the logos... Anyway, we change the sizes of the lifejackets to fit your crew, they have to fit just right if you have kids going out."

"It looks good," Grant said, although he did not believe a word about the engine. The man probably told his friends that the sausage rolls his wife bought in Aldi were made in the same factory as Waitrose. Grant pointed to the fuel tank, which looked like a squashed plastic petrol can, only a little larger. "How many miles can the tank take you?"

"It's hours with boats," the man smirked. "That will run this engine for about three hours."

"And how fast will it go?" DS Clark asked.

"About six knots, which is about seven miles per hour, but you have to watch the tides. If you put in at Falmouth and head for some dinner at The Pandora, and the tide's running a four knot drop, then you'll get there in time for tea," he said with a largely toothless grin.

"The Pandora?" Grant frowned, but he realised it must

have been a restaurant on the river. He'd been thrown about dinner and tea. He'd never heard it used as a replacement for lunch and dinner before. In London if you booked for dinner then you'd get the evening slot and told that tea came in a pot with some cakes.

"It's a pub on the river," DS Clark said. "The Pandora Inn."

"You two aren't together then?" the man asked.

"We're colleagues," Grant said quickly.

"I see..." the man smirked. He had a vision of what these *colleagues* would be doing in the boat. "Anyway, the boat's a good laugh, but it pays to check the conditions out first and not to overload it. The engine's alright, but what you have to remember is we sell five-horsepower Honda and Mariner outboards for between eight hundred and a thousand pounds. This package is an absolute bargain."

"Could it take four adults?"

"You could, I suppose. If you were going a few hundred metres to another boat, using it as a tender." The man shrugged. "It's better suited for a couple of adults and a couple of nippers."

"So, six knots and a favourable tide, and the boat would get you about twenty-one miles?" Grant queried.

The man thought for a moment, but he was looking directly at DS Clark's breasts under the close-fitting blouse as he did the sums, so Grant figured it would take a while. "I suppose," he said eventually. "But if you're running with a good tide, you could get that up to thirty. I wouldn't do it though. I explore the creeks in ours or go out half a mile and drop a fishing line or two. It's a good boat because of the chambers. Stick a hook in one, and you've got nine more full of air. But like I said, great for dinner at The Pandora, but you'd better know what you're doing there."

"Why is that?" Grant asked.

The man took his eyes off DS Clark's breasts for long enough to look at her face. "You know that don't he?" he laughed. "Because thirty people supping wine and pints of beer will be wanting you to fail mooring to the pontoon and take a swim with your clothes on! I'd sit there all bloody day if the wife would let me, just to watch a posh prick in his hundred-grand RIB smack into the pontoon! You'd be alright in this though. These are cheap as chips and people know it, so aren't bothered with you. I watched someone take ten attempts to moor up once in a Bayliner, then his wife drops down to her fanny in the water, just the one leg mind, she gets it back up before the rest of the boat hits and cracks on the pontoon. We all had a good laugh at that one!"

"Sounds delightful," Grant commented. "So, how many of these have you sold?"

"Hundreds."

"Wow. Just from this store?"

"No. We're all online now. We've sold loads on the internet." Grant tried hard to hide his disappointment. The trail was almost impossible, but the internet sales closed the gap from almost to completely. "That's the only one left, so if you want it today, I'll deflate it and pack it up for you and I'll knock off fifty quid. Won't be selling it over the winter months..."

"Thanks for your help," Grant said, turning his back on the man. The man got the message and didn't linger. He walked somewhat dejectedly back down the aisle.

"So?" DS Clark looked at him. "The internet sales make it difficult."

Grant nodded. "There's CCTV on the doors, but none I can see throughout the store."

"They might have hidden cameras?"

"No point. CCTV is a deterrent. They don't want to catch people, merely stop them stealing. I doubt they get much of that anyway. Most of the stuff here is big and bulky. Perhaps the other shop with packets of screws or tools or lightbulbs, but here it's all rope and buoys and rubber fenders. And the cash registers are literally in the doorway."

DS Clark nodded. "Okay. So, we've ascertained that the boat isn't all that sturdy for four adults, but would probably be alright for two adults and two children. The Hafeez family were a party of six..."

"I know. It's inconceivable that they could cross from Calais to Dover, let alone anywhere on the French coast to Cornwall. It's a six-hour ferry crossing from Plymouth to Roscoff. It would take days in a craft like this one. And no motor or fuel tanks were ever found."

"Those oars look a bit flimsy as well," she added.

"What else?"

She frowned, walked around the boat, then looked at Grant and shrugged. "The chambers!" she blurted. "It has ten individual chambers, so a rip might not necessarily sink it."

Grant nodded. "What else?" She thought for a moment, then shrugged again. Grant patted the side of the boat. "It's yellow. It's as bright as the sun. If I were in France, knowing that all that stood between my family and a new life in a country I knew and felt we had a future in, was a hundred or two hundred miles of ocean, I would find something more suitable. More substantial. It wouldn't be a budget rubber boat and it most certainly wouldn't be yellow."

She nodded. "Fair point," she said. "But beggars can't be choosers."

"Exactly," Grant said. "And despite war in their country, and despite the terrible humanitarian crisis, I have dug a little further. Done DCI Warleggan's job for him, so to speak. The Hafeez family were not beggars. Far from it. Qasim Hafeez withdrew the Syrian pound equivalent to two-hundred and sixty-eight thousand pounds Stirling from various accounts, as the war in Syria took hold and it started to look like it would not be a short-term uprising, like others had been during much of the Arab Spring. He sold off assets for cash as well. The Hafeez family were middle-class and well educated. They came from money. They had more than I'll ever earn or could dream of putting aside. This entire refugee crisis has dehumanised people, objectified them. Pricks like DCI Warleggan see people as illegal immigrant scum. But what if the tables were turned? What if the British government waged all-out war on its people because we were unhappy with the way they ran things. What if the army, the RAF and the Royal Navy bombed us all until we supported them completely? Imagine the SAS going in house to house to kill *dissidents*. Now we can't leave our homes, we can't work, we can't buy food..." He shook his head. "Unthinkable, isn't it?" She looked thoughtful and he could tell she hadn't given it much thought until now. Grant hit the side of the boat with his fist and shook his head. "No. The Hafeez family did not set out in that boat," Grant said. "And I don't think they set out on their own from France at all."

Chapter Nine

Grant unfolded a map and spread it out between them in the front seats of the car. He found the approximate area with Falmouth at the bottom left corner. "Go on then, DS Clark, show me where the Pandora Inn is."

"What has it got to do with the case?"

"Nothing. But I'm bloody starving and haven't eaten since my three bites on a barbecued rib last night."

"I don't know if I should..."

"Oh, bloody hell, Clark! It's a bit of lunch," he said and started the car. "I've got it covered."

"Okay," she relented. "Just lunch?"

"What else?"

"Of course, lunch," she said and opened out the map further. She looked a little flustered, as she ran her finger across the map. "It's here. But we don't need the map, I can direct you."

Grant studied the map for a moment. "So, The Point and Loe Creek are over the next two headlands?"

"Yes," she said.

"Trenvarth Manor backs down onto the creek."

"So?"

He did not reply as he folded the map and dropped it into her foot well. "Right. Out of here and right towards Redruth, yes?"

"Yes," she said.

She sat back in her seat and seemed to relax. Her window was open a little and the wind came through and pressed the blouse closer to her skin. If that was possible. Grant glanced at her, but he needed to remain professional. Although he had only recently met her - with the exception of last night's farcical interview with DCI Warleggan - he liked what he saw. DS Lucy Clark was sharp, intelligent and attractive. The full package. He glanced at his face in the rear-view mirror. What would she think of him? Ten years older, greying ever-so-slightly at the temples, his eyes lifeless and grey? Arrogant and bullish? Now covered in bruises with a swollen eye. He mentally shrugged it off. He wasn't twenty anymore and he was fine with that. He had felt stagnant and rutted of late, but he'd had two dates this week already and was falling for another woman, so it wasn't all bad. The thought made him question Mary and her well-being after last night. He had been told that the woman was alright, but he made a note to find her tonight and hear her side of events. Whether it was a past or present lover, whether she could talk more about it, whether he could convince her to be willing to press charges if the two men were ever found. But he wouldn't hold his breath.

Once they left Redruth and then Lanner behind them, the road was clear and swept through wooded areas and small fields and paddocks. It was hilly terrain, and they dipped low in a valley before DS Clark told him to take a left, a 'shortcut' she knew. The road was narrow, and two cars would never pass without someone reluctantly reversing to one of very few passing places cut into the tall hedges. They crossed under the busy A39 through a short granite tunnel and took a steep hill through woods, which meandered through the countryside passing secluded and rather expensive looking houses set back from the road with large gardens and wooded entrances. Clark commented about living here when her lottery numbers came up. Grant would have to agree. His wages were not going to cut it here.

The hill down to Restronguet Creek greeted them with a wonderful view across the water to Restronguet Point. The tide was high, and the sun glistened upon the surface of the water. Boats were moored in the middle of the river and swans glided peacefully between them.

Grant swung into the carpark and was lucky enough to see a car reversing out of a space. He gave the driver room, then drove in and parked. As he opened the door and got out, he noticed that the car park was almost full.

"It gets busy here," DS Clark said, as if reading his thoughts. "Lots of people park and walk down to Mylor. They won't all be eating."

The pub itself was eighteenth century and dark with a thatched roof and small windows. Grant skimmed his head on the roof and flinched, thankful that a padded cushion had been fixed in place. He hovered at the bar, DS Clark catching him up. "Soda water and lime, please," he asked.

The barman looked expectantly at Clark. "Make that two," she said, then turned to Grant. "I'd have a wine, but being on duty and all..."

He nodded in agreement. Duty was always his favourite excuse. Duty and driving. And the gym.

Sixty-days...

The waiting staff bustled through with plates of food. Grant eyed a huge sandwich which looked to be filled with crab. It looked good. He pulled a menu out from a rack in front of the till and opened it up. The drinks were placed on the bar and the barman asked if they wanted anything else. Grant ordered the vast crab sandwich and DS Clark hurried with her choice, feeling the pressure to pay. Despite needing a table number outside, Grant pointed to a table through the window and paid with cash. They walked out with their drinks and were about to sit, when a couple moved from a table on the pontoon.

"That'll do," he said.

"You'll play havoc with their ordering system."

"Well, they'll have to use their initiative," he commented flatly and led the way down the steep wooden walkway and onto the pontoon. As he sat down at the picnic table, he watched a boat slow its revs and steer a course straight for them.

"This is what the bloke at the marine supplies outlet was talking about," DS Clark said and sipped some of her drink.

Grant watched, as did forty other people. Some put down their cutlery to watch. Another took out their phone and started to film. Grant shook his head. "Voyeuristic bastards," he said, but continued to watch all the same.

The boat slowed and came in on a large arc. The man at the helm was in his late-fifties and the woman Grant assumed to be his wife stood on the prow with a rope at the ready. The boat glided right up to the pontoon and the man throttled back and engaged reverse. The engine changed pitch and the boat stopped dead in the water. The man switched off the engine and the woman threw the rope to a man who had stood up from his table and offered a hand.

She stepped off the boat and thanked the man as he wound the rope tightly around a cleat. The man at the helm leapt down and nodded thanks. The onlookers turned back to their drinks and meals and paused conversations, but there was an air of disappointment. Professionalism was not rewarded with this crowd.

"Didn't go as well as that for me and John," DS Clark said dryly.

"Your ex?"

She smiled. "He has a large boat. Half as big again as that one." She nodded towards the sleek and expensive-looking craft. "He was a bit throttle-happy at the best of times. He came in too fast. Shouted at me, but I didn't know what the hell I was doing, didn't know a thing about boats, and I got in a mess with the ropes. He hit the pontoon so hard people's meals ended up on the deck. He smashed the front of the boat in..."

"Prow," Grant smiled. "You're not kidding you know nothing about boats!"

"Shut up!" she laughed. She looked up as a waiter drew near. "That's us!" she called out. "Two crab sandwiches and a bowl of chips... sorry, we moved table..."

The waiter put down the round plastic tray and off-loaded the meals, along with a bucket full of cutlery, napkins and some condiments. When he left to clear another table, they both picked up their doorstop sandwiches and ate quietly.

"So, Mary Hocking..." DS Clark ventured. "You're an item?"

Grant shook his head, a little too adamantly. "We got chatting at the local pub. We had a date afterwards in Truro. She popped round with Chinese food last night. But it was a misunderstanding. She thought I had invited her, but I had said I wanted a quiet night in with a takeaway."

"Jesus. I was just asking, Casanova..." she smiled.

"Well, I..." he stopped. He simply bit into more of the sandwich. If he filled his mouth with food, he wouldn't make more of an idiot of himself. He underestimated the amount of crème fraiche, and a good dollop went onto his shirt. He scraped the excess with the clean blade of his unused knife and tutted loudly. "Sorry about that..."

DS Clark dipped the edge of her paper napkin into her lime and soda and reached over and dabbed at it. She looked up at him and then said, "Sorry, I don't know why I did that..." She looked away, sipped some of her drink.

"Thanks," he said light heartedly. "I'm such a boy sometimes, women just end up mothering me..."

"Mary Hocking," she said. "Did she try to mother you?"

Grant shook his head. "I don't think so. Do you know her?"

"Why?"

"You seem to have an opinion on her."

"I do?"

He shrugged. "Just sounded like that."

"Sorry, unprofessional."

"You're not a doctor, you're a copper," he said. "If you have an opinion, get it out in the open."

"No, I..."

"Spit it out. Shit, one date and a misunderstanding. Two kisses."

"There were kisses?"

"I'm irresistible, what can I say?" he smiled.

"I knew her from holidaying down here. She's the same age, give or take."

"And she got about? Shit, I'm divorced with a child I don't see. We all have a past."

"You have a child?"

"Yes. Is that a problem for you?"

"No. Why would it be?"

"Because you're acting like you're interested, and it's only been a morning, but I'm as interested in you as it's possible to be," he said, glancing at his watch. "After three hours and twenty-seven minutes..."

She laughed. "Well, we could see how this pans out and take it from there."

"Sounds like a plan." He smiled. "Of course, if you feel pressured by a senior officer, feel free to call your federation rep."

"I'll be okay," she said, then chuckled. "Well, you can make your own judgements on *Ms* Hocking."

"Perhaps," he said non-committedly. "But I want to find her and see if she knows anything about last night, or if she's okay, despite DCI Warleggan's word on the matter."

"Well, I might know where to find her," she said.

Chapter Ten

The road from Mylor towards the Point like much of the area was lined with trees and interspersed by paddocks and fields. The hedges were high and covered with foliage, and for much of the route the trees topping the hedges grew over the road in arches, their branches meeting and forming a tunnel of thick green leaves. The sun shone through the canopy, occasionally blinding Grant in its glare when the foliage thinned. He wished he'd brought some sunglasses with him. He looked across at DS Clark, who with her dark, glossy hair, dark Gucci sunglasses and tight-fitting white blouse, looked like chic personified. She swept a lock of hair away from her face, the breeze billowing through her half-open window.

Grant slowed as they approached a grand entrance on their right. The signage was carved elegantly into a slab of granite at least six-feet square. He downshifted the Alfa Romeo and slowed to a crawl. Beside the sign was a colourful banner promoting an event for a local charity tomorrow night. It advertised champagne on arrival, a free bar, an auction, canapés and a house tour. The main event was a raffle draw for a car supplied by a local BMW and Mini dealership. There was a number to call and a weird black and white symbol in a box.

"Trenvarth Manor," she said.

"Their land backs down all the way to the Creek?"

"That's right," she nodded. "Why are you so interested?"

"Just something I need to check out later," he replied as he took out his phone and took a couple of pictures of the sign.

"Just scan the QR box," DS Clark said. "It will take you right to their website."

He looked at her, then to his iPhone. "I wondered what those things were."

"You're kidding, right?" She laughed. "They're all over London." She snatched the phone out of his hand lined the QR box up so that it filled the screen. "That's it," she said, then looked at the phone, disappointed. "Can't help the Cornish phone signal though. You've got no bars."

"I barely have since I've been here."

"Well, when you get enough for internet access click on the QR box..." She showed him before passing the phone back to him. "It will tell you all about the event being held at Trenvarth Manor. Either that, or the charity Roebuck is raising money for."

"Roebuck?"

"Claude Roebuck is the Lord of the Manor, or he likes to think he is. He's not really a lord, or *any* type of nobility, but he acts like it. He came from money but made a load more on his own. Filthy rich. He owns other properties, mainly holiday homes. He's responsible for keeping many of the Cornish out of homes and driving them to where property is more affordable, according to some."

"And is he?"

"Doubtful," she scoffed. "He owns some of the most luxurious homes down here. They aren't the sort of properties to keep low earners or key workers off the property ownership ladder. But his properties still manage to piss people off. They are usually big and modern looking – a celebration of glass and stainless steel and wood – and they stay empty for half the year, so that kills local trade and communities in the winter months."

Grant nodded. "There's quite a few of those empty already on the Point and along to Loe Creek. I thought they would be rented up until October half term at least."

"I think the seasons are getting shorter. Parents can't take their kids out of school either side of the holidays. Businesses are suffering for sure. I think affordable cottages do okay, but some of those houses on the creek rent out for eight grand a week."

"What?" Grant shook his head. "Well, they should all make their investment money back soon," he said. "So, Roebuck makes that kind of money?"

"All day long. He owns care homes across the county as well. There was some controversy a few years ago. He does, or at least *did*, deals with the people going into his homes, along the lines of buying their houses and releasing the equity which he would then off-set against their care fees."

"And the families objected?"

"Exactly. He made his accounts available, and it showed good value in terms of ancillary care, but the houses were woefully undervalued, and he paid far less than market rate. He was the silent partner in a letting and estate agency. The properties ended up being let out or sold through the agency, but they came into the company at a far higher investment price than the old people were given. Roebuck couldn't account for the deficit and ended up paying a fortune in personal taxes. It was all over the local papers, but he's done a lot of charity work since, and everyone loves him again." The drove onto the point and DS Clark pointed left towards the river. "Down that road," she said. "See the big house on the quay?"

"Yes."

"That's it."

"Really?"

"Really," she said. "I'll wait in the car. Don't get *too* reacquainted."

He smiled and parked up behind a ten-year-old convertible Mini Cooper. He got out and shut the door without saying anything. In truth, he was a little embarrassed. He hadn't thrown himself into anything before the date with Mary. And he had felt comfortable kissing her last night. But something did not feel right, and that only came about when he had spent time with Lucy Clark. He had never had relationships with colleagues, but this time he seemed to be able to justify it somehow. He had only known her for a matter of hours, but he felt something he had never felt before. Not even with his wife, the woman he had vowed to be with forever. He thought of spending more time with DS Clark. The idea appealed to him. And it wasn't just the fact that it would be driving DCI Warleggan crazy.

There were an open set of wrought iron gates, painted black with gold paint on the spear-tips. It looked a little too Cheshire for Grant. For the rest of the village too. There was a 'for rent' sign attached to the railings by a company called Keith & Davey. The gravel on the drive was grey slate chips that were thickly applied. The borders were weeded and heavily planted out with flowers and plants and the earth was covered with bark chips. It looked as if a gardener had worked hard on the beds over the summer. Grant stood and looked at the house. It was large and square, and constructed from granite, the cement new and repointed. The roof looked new as well and the windows were triple-glazed and from the discreet tubing above, looked to be self-cleaning. Mary Hocking worked part-time shifts at a local pub. There was no way she would afford this, and even if she could, through inheritance or windfall or even hard work, a few hours at minimum wage wasn't going to make a bit of difference.

He rang the doorbell and stood back. He could see a figure moving behind the quarter section of smoked glass in the dark oak door. It looked like Mary, and she seemed to stop and look at the wall before opening the door. Grant realised it had been a mirror. He stood back a step and smiled. "Glad to see you're..." he paused. She was wearing a figure-hugging leather dress that would have been an effort to get into, and it was so short that it barely covered her knickers. "...okay," he added, still staring at the dress.

She looked visibly shocked when she saw him. She managed to regain some composure but frowned and looked past him warily. "Grant?" she said. "What are you doing here?"

Grant recovered quickly, or thought he had. His face still questioned her appearance. "Sorry, I wanted to see if you were alright, after last night."

Again, she looked right past him. "Fine, just a misunder-standing, that's all."

Grant smiled, but his expression dropped almost as quickly. He walked in, barging her out of the way. She over-reacted, feigning an act of losing her balance and looking surprised. He wasn't having any of it. "Bullshit!" he snapped. "Shut the fucking door and listen to me..."

She did as he ordered, stood back from the door and smoothed the dress over her hips. It was a challenge to breathe and keep her intimate areas covered. "I..."

"Shut up!" Grant glared. "Last night, two men threatened me with a shotgun and tied me up. They beat the living crap out of me, and the last I saw, you were being manhandled out of the house with the threat of a man taking you for sex, *apparently* against your will. You don't get to pick and choose. I want to know who they were, and you need to make a statement. Which you can do tomorrow morning at nine o'clock, to me in person, at Camborne police station."

"But..."

"I said, shut up!" he snapped again. "DCI Warleggan. You know him, right?"

"Yes."

"What happened when the guy took you away?"

She shrugged. "Nothing."

"He said he was going to *give you one*," Grant said. "You were kicking and screaming, that would suggest he was going to rape you."

She shook her head. "No."

"So, he didn't rape you or sexually assault you?"

"No."

"What then?"

"He said that he was there to warn you off. That I should go and forget all about it."

"And that was that? He let you go?"

"He did."

"Well, thanks for your concern," he said coldly. "You didn't think to see if I was okay?"

"I called the cops!"

"And said what?"

"That there'd been a fight."

"A fight? It was more than a bloody fight, Mary. They had a gun, they tied me up..."

"Look, I called the police, but I don't want to get involved."

"Did you know the men?" She hesitated. Grant watched her closely. "Well, did you?"

"No."

Grant turned and walked out of the hallway and into a spacious lounge. It looked out on the creek, just a mile closer to the sea than the Hemingway House. "This is a multi-million-pound view," he said. "How are you here?"

"Thanks!"

"You're a barmaid," he retorted. "You work part-time."

"It belongs to a friend," she conceded quietly, solemnly. "He's letting me stay while I get straight."

"Where are your things?"

"What?"

"There's nothing *in* here," Grant walked out into the kitchen. She followed, tottering on her high heels. He looked around the kitchen, opened the fridge. "Nothing. Not even milk. The fridge isn't even switched on."

"Get out!" she snapped venomously. Then added, "How did you know I was here? Who told you?"

"A colleague."

"That bitch Lucy Clark," she laughed. "I thought so. DS *Bloody* Clark."

"You've got history then?"

"And then some," she seethed. "She needs to let it go."

"What?"

"Ask her," she said. "I'm done talking. I'll make that statement tomorrow, until then..." She walked back out to the hallway and stood by the door, her hand resting on the door handle. She waited for Grant to catch up. "Goodbye…"

He looked at her incredulously. "DCI Warleggan told you not to get involved, not to make a statement, didn't he? Why?"

"Ask him yourself. I'm done."

"He knows you're a prostitute?"

She glared at him, but he could see the sadness in her eyes, and there were tears forming making them glossy and vulnerable. "Just go, please…" she said quietly. "I thought I saw a way out of all this with someone like you. Someone who didn't know what I have had to do, someone who took me for what they saw and liked me… And now you're standing there, *judging* me. Well life isn't always a bed of roses, and you don't get to know people's pasts or secrets, or what they've had to do. Not if they don't want you to."

"Mary…"

"Just go!" she snapped and turned around, facing the door. She was crying. She cupped her face, and the skirt was so short it that rode up to reveal a flash of red silk underneath. Grant put a hand on her shoulder, and she flinched away. "Stop it, leave me alone," she said sadly.

Grant opened the door and stepped out. The door slammed behind him, and he felt the wind from it against his back. He stepped down onto the gravel and walked back to the car without looking back. As he reached the car, a man in his fifties slinked around the hedge and railings and walked across the gravel driveway. He was overweight and balding. He fidgeted nervously on the doorstep. He rapped on the door and stood back. Grant watched as the door opened, Mary out of sight behind it, and the man stepped inside. The door closed and Grant got back into the car.

"You're welcome," DS Clark said.

"What for?"

"You swerved a messy situation with that one. Good job it ended at a Chinese takeaway and a kiss."

"She doesn't like you much," he commented.

"She said that? I'm hurt," she smirked.

"How do you know each other?"

"I'm a police officer. She's a whore. Our paths have crossed."

"She said you should just *let it go*. What's that about?"

"No idea. She doesn't like being nicked, that's all."

"Are you going to nick her now?" Grant asked. "That guy could do with a shake down."

"Oh, he's *getting* that for sure."

"I meant arrested. I'll bet he's married with kids. What makes someone risk all of that?"

"Sex."

"Figures," Grant shrugged. "I hope it's worth it. Losing a family makes you rethink just about everything in your life."

"And that happened to you?"

Grant started to the car and reversed back out onto the road. He said nothing, but he felt there was much to ask. He just needed to get the questions in the right order.

Chapter Eleven

"So, what are we doing at your house?" DS Clark laughed. "It's a bit too soon for me. I just meant we'd have a drink when we've finished your investigation, see where it goes."

Grant looked at her and smiled. "I want to check something out."

"I bet you do."

"Come on, you'll see," he said. "How are you with boats?"

"I told you, I don't know what I'm doing and don't know which end of the rope to hold."

"Well, it's not a thirty-odd-foot power boat, and this isn't the Pandora Inn," he said and opened his door.

DS Clark followed. They walked around the side of the house and out onto the lawn. The tide was still coming in and three swans glided in with it. The sun was high above them casting a hue of gold across the water. "This is gorgeous," she said.

"Pretty idyllic, isn't it?" He looked out across the water.

"I don't miss London when I stand out here and look at this."

"You could put in for a transfer," she quipped. "Look at it every day."

He smiled. "It's not my house, remember? I got cleaned out during my divorce. Unless I get some compensation for my injury, I'd be in a two-bed new-build semi on an estate someplace, wouldn't see a view anything like this in the morning..."

She chuckled. "Well, a view is always free. Just take an interesting route to work. So what boat is it, and what the hell are we doing?"

Grant stopped and looked at the upturned boat. He wasn't sure what it was, but he went with a big rowing boat. He pointed at the hull. "That."

"That?"

"Yes."

"I've never rowed."

"Good. That makes two of us," he said. "But it can't be all that difficult."

"Famous last words..."

They caught hold of each end of the boat and turned it over. It was heavy and cumbersome, but once it tilted so far, it spun freely and slipped out of their hands, the hull dropping heavily onto the area of chippings that had been laid aside for the boat and the remains of two broken-looking canoes. The quay was a three-foot drop to the shingle and mud beach, but at high tide Grant had noticed it was over two feet deep with water. They lowered the boat down onto the beach and Grant jumped down, instantly sinking to his ankles in the mud. He pulled a face and DS Clark laughed. She kicked off her leather boots and rolled her tight jeans over her calves.

"That mud stinks now that you've broken it up!"

She was right. Grant screwed his face up at the stench of rotted fish and vegetation and dragged the boat into the water. DS Clark picked up the oars and handed one to him. Grant got into the boat first, his muddy shoes streaking the fowl-smelling mud over the cream-coloured hull. He positioned himself on the forward bench and steadied the vessel with a hand on both sides. It did nothing to right the tilt of the boat as DS Clark got in and slipped down onto the rear bench. She fumbled with her oar and the boat drifted out into the river.

"Here, give me the other oar," he said.

He got both into the rowlocks and started to row. It didn't go well and for the first five minutes the boat went in every direction but where he wanted it to go, and he caught the occasional oar on either the muddy bottom, or just got it wrong and the oar slipped out of the rowlocks and left them spinning in circles.

"Can I have a go?"

"You think you can do better?"

"I think it would be impossible to do any worse..."

He pulled the oars back in and set about transferring his weight across to the rear seat as she did the same. Unsurprisingly, this was difficult as well and the boat almost capsized when his three and a half stone premium on her weight almost sent him over the side. Now in each other's seats, DS Clark set about placing the oars in the rowlocks while Grant clutched onto both sides. To his annoyance, she skulled the boat around and rowed in a fairly straight line towards the far bank.

"The world and his dog hate a show-off," he said.

She smiled, the sun lighting up her face. He noticed her eyes were as blue as the sky and her hair was darker than pitch. She had a slight tan, which brought out her eyes. She was quite possibly one of the most beautiful women he had ever seen. And she seemed more so the longer he was in her company. "I take it we're heading for the jetty?" she asked.

"We are."

"Makes sense. I wasn't sure where you were going."

"I was just familiarising myself with the river," he said. "Getting an idea what the tide was doing." He grinned. She rowed well, her breasts straining against the material of the blouse. Her arms were toned, and he could tell that her stomach and core were strong. "You've done this before, DS Clark."

"Do you still want to ask me out for a drink when we're done?"

"I might. It's only been a day."

"Well, call me Lucy," she said. "Can you do that, *Superintendent*?"

"*Acting* Superintendent."

"I have a feeling you'll be DCI very soon."

"Why?" He looked shocked.

"I don't think you make things ride easily for you."

"No?"

"No."

He shrugged. "Easy come, easy go."

"Did your wife call you Grant?"

"Sometimes."

"What's your Christian name?"

"Don't go there."

She smiled. "I could look it up..."

"You won't be getting it from me."

"So, what did your wife call you, then?"

"Bastard, most of the time..." He shrugged. "And with good reason, I suppose."

She smiled awkwardly and did not press it further. The jetty loomed and she took the oars out of the water. The boat glided slowly towards it, then nudged the timber edge. "It's deep here," she said. "Look. The bottom is six-feet deep, I'd say."

"The bank is sheer. That's how they got a bigger boat in here last night."

"Who did?"

"I saw a boat come in at dusk. You see that tree?" He pointed at the submerged tree, and she nodded. "That hid the boat from view."

"What kind of boat?"

"A fishing boat. On old and battered thing. It had two men in the cabin. When I looked with binoculars, people were getting off it. I increased the focus and light setting and saw a man looking back at me with a pair of binoculars."

"Creepy."

"It was, but in the next instant, Mary Hocking came in with a takeaway and switched on the light. Naturally I couldn't see anything with the light on and by the time she switched it back off, the people and the man with the binoculars had disappeared."

"And you never saw these men again?"

"Oh, I think I did," he said. "I'm sure they were the two men who threatened me with the gun and attacked me."

"Why didn't you say this last night?"

Grant scoffed. "I could tell he was a lousy copper. His line about Mary told me that. As far as I was concerned, the woman had been sexually assaulted and taken against her will."

"I'm sure she's had worse."

Grant looked at her. "I'm sure she has," he said seriously. "But there is always more to a situation than what can be seen at face value."

"I know, but..."

"No. That woman sells her body, that much is clear. I didn't see it coming, but I don't know any more than that," Grant said. He looked at her, a feeling of uncertainty rising within him. Her comment had been callous. But then again, he'd thrown his hat into the ring with a woman he barely knew. He'd never done that before. What did he expect? He didn't even know DS Lucy Clark. If anything, he knew Mary Hocking better. "Look, you clearly have history with this woman, other than nicking her for prostitution, so tell me."

"It's nothing," she answered curtly. "I knew of her when I holidayed down here. She was always knocking around Falmouth. I saw her around at the beaches, then when I was older, at the pubs and places older kids hang out. When I first arrested her, it was awkward for her. A little for me, too."

"And that's it?"

"I don't like people selling themselves," she added, "There's no need."

Grant stepped out of the boat and DS Clark scowled as she was left rocking and trying to stash the oars. "Need and want."

"What?"

"Everybody wants sex. It's a basic human emotion. We all want it for different reasons. To feel loved, to feel secure, to feel liberated. To feel in control, to feel dominated. Or just because it feels good," he said. "But in all my years as a police officer, I have never met anybody who truly wanted to sell their body for money. Not when you scratch away at the reasoning for doing it."

"Easy money."

"Is it? I'm sure if Brad Pitt came round and wanted to get his rocks off then plenty of women would jump at the chance…"

"Brad Pitt! You're showing your age!"

"Alright, that bloke off Poldark then," he said curtly. "Or Eddie Redmayne or Jude Law. But women in the sex industry don't get that. They get halitosis and missing teeth, fat and smelly beasts with hygiene problems and perverse desires. They can't simply say no when they open the door to them."

She shrugged. "It's their career choice. Mary Hocking could work on a supermarket checkout, but she chooses to spread her legs for a hundred quid a shot."

"I've known crime syndicates force women into that sort of work. There are immigrants who have their passports held and are forced to work for free to pay off the debt for being brought over. The sex industry is full of modern-day slaves with little choice."

"But Mary has choices. She just makes bad ones, that's all." She pulled down the legs of her jeans and put her boots back on.

Grant shrugged. He could see that history was unforgiving and made a note to delve deeper in Mary Hocking's past. He would need the national crime database for the task, but he figured tomorrow would be the time for that. He had a meeting with Mary at nine, he just hoped she would attend voluntarily.

"So, what are we looking for?" DS Clark asked, sensing it was time for a change in topic. "The boat brought people in, you say?"

"There were people on the jetty. All sizes. I only caught a fleeting glance. It could have been women or children. There were only two men on deck who piloted the boat in."

"Smuggling, I'd bet," she said. "It goes on. Always has. It's just the booty that has changed. Drugs is the biggest and most valuable commodity. Everything from weed to ecstasy to cocaine. Drugs are rife in Cornwall."

"Really?"

"County lines is a major worry," she replied. "There's a big drug recreational scene down here. Everybody smoked weed when I was a kid. Especially the surfers and beach bums. And then there's the rave scene where ecstasy is the drug of choice. Now it's as likely to be speed or ice. Heroin is back in favour again."

Grant shook his head. "I'd never have thought that."

"It's not all pasties and ice cream down here," she retorted. "Cigarettes and tobacco are the next most smuggled contraband, and booze is third. Vodka makes good sense. There are a still a lot of Polish here, they love the stuff. But pub landlords buy up anything and decant it into the branded optics. It's not so common now, not smuggled at least, because the budget supermarkets offer spirits so cheap, the landlords buy that instead. It goes on more than you'd think."

Grant looked around, focusing his attention on the ground. There was a lot of mud and footprints. The jetty led to a path. The path looked well-used, like a coastal footpath, carved through the ground, but the wooden boards of the jetty were clean. One-way traffic. "Notice anything?"

DS Clark studied the area. She looked at him and shook her head.

"The jetty is clean. People have moved in one direction. Or at least, a high proportion have."

She nodded. "Well, let's follow the path."

They walked single file, Grant taking the lead. The path wound around the bank of the creek, then angled straight up a hill, so steep that Grant could almost touch the ground in front of him as he climbed. After fifty metres or so the path went through a cluster of trees which gradually turned into a small wood. He turned to DS Clark. "I thought they might have been poaching."

"Well, this is Roebuck's land, and the Trenvarth Estate hosts shoots of all types. Pigeons in the summer, duck and other wildfowl in the autumn and pheasant drives in the winter. Some of the locals work as beaters, many get paid in pheasants. The estate also shoots the various species of deer year-round, depending on what's legal and in season."

"And this is definitely his land?"

"Yes. It runs right down to the bank opposite the Point. That jetty has to be his."

"It would be a worthwhile venture to sail up the river and shoot a deer. I suppose they are large and could be butchered up and sold easily. There was venison on the menu at the local pub. It would be worth selling it to kitchens via the backdoor."

"Absolutely," she said. "But you're not down from London to look into poaching and selling a bit of venison."

"No, I'm not."

"And the tie-in is the dead Syrian family."

"That's what I think."

She hesitated, her eyes catching something in the grass. Then she said quietly, "Oh Jesus..."

"What?"

"You know it's not smuggling, don't you? Not contraband at least."

"That's what I'm going to prove."

"You think it's people trafficking, don't you," she stated flatly.

"I'm pretty sure it is, yes."

She walked off the path a few feet and bent down. She picked something up and walked over to him. She held it out and Grant took it from her and looked at it. It was a tatty, worn teddy bear. Part of the arm had torn, and stuffing was visible between the stretched threads and torn fabric. "I think you've found something," he said. He brought it close to his nose and smelled it, sniffing deeply. It smelled of something other than the woods, not yet taking on the musty, dank smell of the foliage and mud and grass.

It still smelled of its owner.

Chapter Twelve

DS Clark put the teddy in an evidence bag that she carried in her handbag. She marked the label with a marker pen. TM1. Trenvarth Manor, one. She dated it and put her name on it. She was about to enter Grant's name, but he told her not to. She frowned, but he shook his head.

"I'm down here ruffling feathers," he said. "You take the credit." It was a good enough reason, but Grant conceded it was not the only reason. But he couldn't tell her. Not yet.

"You think they trafficked children?"

He shook his head. "I think they trafficked a family."

"The Hafeez family? You think they were being trafficked?"

"Not exactly..." he broke off, dropped to the ground as a huge clump of soil splattered over their faces and a gunshot sang out across the valley. It echoed sharply unlike the gunshots he had heard previously during his stay.

"What the hell?" DS Clark cried out. "Someone just shot at us!"

There was another gunshot, another clump of soil. It

was close to Grant's feet. He rolled over and pulled DS Clark down into a culvert. There were bones and animal fur in the culvert, and it spread out from a large hole. Grant realised it was a badger's sett.

"You there!" a voice called out. "What the hell are you doing on this land?"

Grant chanced a peek and saw a tall, thin man dressed in tweed striding towards them. He was accompanied by a shorter, stockier man who wore a cheap and tatty green jacket and ripped jeans, which would have once been blue, but now looked the colour of mud. The taller man carried a hunting rifle with a scope. The stockier man carried a shotgun, its barrels broken over his arm.

Grant took out his warrant card and held it up. "Put the gun down!"

"I'll do nothing of the sort!" the taller man snorted. "Who the hell are you and what are you doing on Trenvarth Manor Estate?"

Grant nodded for DS Clark to get up. He turned to the men and said again, "Put the guns down. I'm a police officer, this is my colleague."

"You're trespassing without a warrant," the taller man said. "I'm Claude Roebuck and I own this land."

"You shot at us," Grant said. "Now put the guns down, or I'll take them off you."

The stockier man snapped the shotgun shut and the barrels drifted up towards Grant's midriff. "No, I don't think you will..."

"Now, now Bunt..." Roebuck said. "I think we gave the inspector here a scare when we mistook him for a red hind on my land." He pulled back the bolt action and ejected a large brass cartridge into his hand. He rested the rifle on the ground at his feet. The man called Bunt opened the barrels of the side-by-side shotgun and rested it in the crook of his elbow. He stared at Grant, a smirk on his lips.

Grant looked at the man's hands and forearms. Tattooed and tanned like the man holding the shotgun last night. The shotgun looked the same too. The blueing worn and shiny at end of the barrels. He looked at the man, watched his eyes carefully. He wasn't close enough to see if the iris of his right eye had bled into the white. "I didn't recognise you," he said icily. "Without your balaclava."

The man smiled. "Don't know what you mean, officer."

"I think you do."

Roebuck coughed. "You know each other?"

Bunt shook his head. "Never seen *he* before..."

"You sound the same."

"Well, *we's* all sound the same to you *emmets*..."

Grant looked at Roebuck. "Mind if I take a look at your rifle?" He didn't wait for a reply, simply bent down and picked it up. He shouldered it and aimed at the point he had first seen the two men. He lowered the rifle, looked back at Roebuck. "That scope looks pretty clear to me. You must be half blind if you thought both DS Clark and I looked like deer."

"You're a sergeant now?" Bunt said with a smirk. "Well, the promotion ladder is open for women to climb here. They'll let anybody up, if *they's* give something in return, I *s'pose*."

"You shut your face! You odious little..."

"DS Clark!" Grant snapped. "That's enough..." He looked back at Roebuck. "I was saying that you took two shots at people thinking they were a deer."

"Well, it's the light, you see," Roebuck caught hold of the fore-stock and pulled, but Grant gripped harder. "I didn't expect trespassers on my land."

"I think a visit from Firearms Licensing may be in order. Just to check you have everything in place. Like your DSC is valid. You need that to stalk deer, I gather."

"We run professional shoots here, Bunt is in charge of all that."

Bunt nodded. "Can't tell us a bloody thing..."

Grant frowned and interrupted him. "Well, you thought I was a red hind. It's illegal to shoot female red deer this time of year. It's fallow deer and roe deer males in England and Wales. Just a quick Google earlier. With such a simple mistake, I imagine you're making many more."

"I've only made one mistake lately," Bunt said.

"You bet your life you have," Grant said coldly. "And when you make another, I'll see it's the last you ever make..."

Chapter Thirteen

"Well, that could have gone better."

"I think it went pretty well myself," Grant said. He stepped into the boat, eased himself to the back. "You're rowing, by the way."

"Naturally." She sat down on the jetty and eased herself down into the boat and onto the seat. The boat rocked, but Grant was holding onto the edge of the jetty, and it was far more stable than it had been both on the other side and in the middle of the creek. "And why didn't you mention the teddy bear?"

"Time and place. It wasn't looking too safe with the guns. And besides, if something is amiss then I want to hold the cards." He pushed away from the jetty once she got the oars into the water. "They shot at us on purpose. I saw the clarity of that rifle scope and it was a quality piece. If anything, they would have seen so much more than merely a figure moving. Roebuck could have read the front page of a newspaper with that scope at that range."

"Are you sure it was the rifle that fired and not the shotgun?"

"Absolutely. The sound for one. And no spread pattern meant it was a bullet, not shotgun shot." Grant looked at her as she rowed. "So, what's with you and Bunt? You know him. Or at least, he knows you and has formed a pretty strong opinion of you."

"Remember I told you my ex took me apart in the courtroom and got a man off a rape charge? Well, that man was Pete Bunt."

Grant was silent for a moment, looked at her and said, "I'm convinced he was one of the men from last night. He had similar tattoos, from what I remember. The shotgun looked a match too, and he all but hinted as much. He thinks he's untouchable for some reason."

"That will be Roebuck's influence."

"So, who is he?"

"Sometime fisherman, welfare scammer, slaughterman and general waster. Now he works as a gamekeeper, groundsman and general dog's body for Claude Roebuck."

"And he was the man you were prosecuting? This was the case that cost you your relationship with your lawyer boyfriend?"

"No. It cost my lawyer boyfriend his relationship with me," she corrected him. "It showed me what a scumbag he was and what he would do to win a case."

"Okay. I get the differentiation. But it makes no sense for a high-profile landowner and businessman to employ a man like that." They were approaching the other side of the creek and Grant nodded to her. "Twenty-feet, stop rowing."

She lifted the oars and the boat glided into the beach. There was a foot or so of mud and shingle to step onto. The boat was grounded and not going anywhere. Grant, not caring for his filthy shoes and trouser bottoms, stepped out and into a few inches of water. DS Clark started to unzip her boots, but he stopped her. "I'll lift you if you want," he said. "Save you messing about."

She looked up at him and shrugged. "Okay," she said and stood up.

Grant bent down and put a hand behind her knees, the other around her waist and scissor motioned his arms. She dropped into his arms and looked up at him as he walked out of the water and onto the muddy beach. He looked at her, felt a quickening of his heartbeat as he watched her eyes. He swung her up to the top of the stone quay. She landed nimbly on the grass, and he let go. The moment was over, and he bent down and lifted the prow of the boat up to the quay. "Here, take this," he said and walked around to lift the stern. She pulled and Grant pushed, and the boat slid neatly up the quay and rested still on the grass. The oars were inside. He'd turn the boat over and store it properly another time. For now, he wanted to change his trousers and shoes before he made his next port of call.

Grant led the way through the garden and around the side of the house, letting them in through the front door. He dropped his keys onto the hall table and nodded towards the kitchen. "Get a brew on," he said, kicking his muddy shoes off. "How do you have your coffee?"

"Black," she said.

"Lucky. I haven't got any milk. I'll be down in a minute." He ran up the stairs and tore his trousers off at the top, took off his socks. He took out his wallet and warrant card, his mobile phone and pulled the belt out from the loops. He could hear DS Clark filling the kettle, the water made some noise in the pipes, but he had never known water pressure like it. The tap in the kitchen jumped each time it was shut off. He walked into the bedroom, dropped his things on the bed and took another pair of trousers out of the wardrobe. Dress was a little more casual in Cornwall, so he settled on a pair of tan cargoes and changed his shirt for a light blue one. He rolled the sleeves and wore it open without a tie, taking a tan sports jacket out of the wardrobe for the changeable weather and unpredictable biting wind.

He had been quick, but by the time he got back downstairs, DS Clark had the coffee made. She had taken it into the lounge and was watching the bank on the opposite side of the river.

"We should move quickly," she said.

"We don't have anything concrete." He took the coffee off her and sipped a little, unsurprisingly, it was scalding.

"We have the teddy bear."

"Exactly."

"But with what you saw..."

"What *did* I see?" he paused. "Think as a lawyer. Would the teddy bear be enough for a warrant?"

She shook her head. "Okay, but we need to move. There could be a child, or an entire family..."

"What? Free because they paid to be brought over? It's how it could look, and it's not enough."

"What then?"

"Back to the Hafeez family." Grant perched on the back of the sofa and looked out across the water. The tide was still on the push. "I want to see them."

"What?" she asked, incredulously.

Grant sipped some more coffee and kept his eyes on the glistening water of the creek. "Or more specifically," he paused. "I want to see their grave."

Chapter Fourteen

I t was only five minutes longer than the most direct
route through Falmouth, but at DS Clark's suggestion, Grant had taken the Castle Drive route and
driven past Gyllyngvase Beach. With the stately-looking
hotels to their right and a promenade overlooking the beautiful glistening sea to their left, it reminded Grant of a short
section of Torquay. He thought the sea view to be breath-
taking, with sharp cliffs and smaller bays in the distance.
Three large tankers were moored a mile or so out to sea. DS
Clark had told him that the promenade was an unusual
feature in Cornwall, as she could only think of Penzance
and Mount's Bay as having a promenade to walk along.
They passed a sandy beach at the far end, a café and public
garden, then the road left the beach behind and climbed
through a residential area and DS Clark told him to pull in
and park on the left.

There were far worse places to be eternally laid to rest
than the plots at Swanvale. Edged in trees, the plots set
among neatly mowed grass, with plants growing sporadi-
cally and glimpsing views of the Atlantic Ocean at the next

bay, the site benefited from Falmouth's micro-climate of mild, bright weather all year round. DS Clark informed Grant that St. Ives and Falmouth had more hours of sun and were marginally warmer than anywhere else in Cornwall. She wasn't wrong. The temperature was warmer than it had been back at the point and the sun was high and the sky a deep blue and relatively cloud free.

Grant got out of the car and looked at the main entrance. It was secured by black iron gates. There was a notice board and a list of contacts on the wall.

"Should have called," DS Clark said.

"Now why didn't I think of that..." Grant looked at the man approaching them. He was short and overweight, balding and wore the thickest glasses imaginable. Not the most fortunate fellow, but his smile was intoxicating and as warm as it was possible to be.

"Mister Grant, sorry... Inspector?"

"That'll do," Grant returned the man's smile and opened his warrant card for him to see. It indicated his newly reinstated rank of Detective Chief Inspector, but he wasn't going to go into ranks and protocols. "You must be Alan. Thank you for meeting with us, so late in the day."

"No, no. Always a pleasure to help the police," he said. "Actually, I've never really helped the police before, but it's still a pleasure!"

Grant started walking into the burial gardens, prompting the man to follow and then assume the lead. "Did you not deal with the police after the vandalism to the grave?"

"No," he replied emphatically. "But I was given a log number."

"But nobody followed up with a visit?"

"No."

Grant turned to DS Clark as they walked in the shade of the tree canopies. "Was there talk about the incident?" he asked.

"I didn't hear anything. No investigation as far as I know. The papers ran with the story for a while, but I didn't hear of any police action." She ducked a branch and swiped a lock of hair from her face. "There are under a hundred officers in CID throughout Cornwall. We work out of whichever station is geographically closest to the crime. With many stations closing in favour of non-emergency calls direct to Exeter, we don't rub shoulders too regularly. There are officers I don't see from one month to the next and some I'll never see. We don't get to hear much concerning other cases. Most contact is through email and our internal online bulletin board."

The rounded the path and entered a garden edged in privet bush. Alan stopped; his head bowed. They stopped too, Grant bowed his head in mutual respect, noticed DS Clark looked towards the sea. "Here we are," Alan said quietly.

The plot was covered in fresh earth and there were flowers on top in a sunken vase. They looked fresh, but Grant didn't know what they were. The headstone looked to be marble or polished granite. He suspected the latter given the amount of granite he had seen throughout the county.

"So, you cleaned the headstone off?" Grant asked.

"No, there was no damage to the headstone, detective," Alan sighed. "The people from the Islamic centre at Carnon Downs came down and replaced the vase. They replenished the flowers, and then the Imam held a sort of blessing."

"But the headstone wasn't touched?"

"No."

"What was the extent of the vandalism?" Grant frowned. "Just the broken vase?"

Alan shook his head. "No, I didn't really say it was vandalism," he said, somewhat perplexed. "I said that whoever had done this had tried to dig the grave out properly."

DS Clark pulled a face. It wasn't the prettiest she'd looked all day. "You mean..."

"Yes!" exclaimed Alan. "That's what I said to the other detective. It was as though someone tried to get to the bodies."

"But you said that you didn't deal with the police. You never said you spoke to someone," Grant sighed. "Which is it?"

"I didn't speak to anyone in person," he said. "I called the police when we discovered the damage. I was given a log number." He took out a fold of paper and handed it to Grant. "Here," he said. "It's all on there, date, number and time."

"Right..."

"The other warden who worked here spoke to the police when they came," he said.

"And what did they say?"

"It was just one officer, a detective. He looked around, took some photographs and told John he'd better fill it back in. We called the West Briton newspaper, and they came out and took a picture of the Islamic charity replacing the flowers. We'd filled it in by then. Couldn't have an open grave for all the world to see..."

"Well, how far did they dig down?"

"Four feet or so."

"Four feet!" Grant shook his head. "Well, that wasn't

just petty vandalism. That would have been damned hard work, organised too."

"I know, that's what we said. John came in early, saw the gates had been broken open and a van was parked outside. He heard noise inside and went in to have a look see."

Grant shook his head. It wasn't the most sensible thing he'd heard. But it wasn't the worse. "How early?" Grant asked.

"About five. John was up with the lark. He would do a few chores here then go back to Flushing and go out in his boat, set his crab and lobster pots or bring in the ones he'd had soaking. Then he'd come back and work part of the day. We keep our hours quite flexible. He shouted at them and obviously disturbed them while they were digging. He said they'd had a scuffle, but I think he exaggerated a bit. He must have chased them off though."

"Could you give me his number? I think it's high time I got his version of events."

Alan cast his head for a moment. He looked back at them both and shrugged. "I'm sorry, John Trevithick had an accident. He got caught up with one of his pots and fell overboard," he said sadly. "He was a typical fisherman, not a great swimmer, but he must have snared his leg in the line or something, because he was pulled overboard and under the surface."

"When was this?" DS Clark asked. She glanced at Grant, then looked back at the small, round man.

"The day after."

They were silent for a moment. Alan out of respect for his dead colleague, Grant and DS Clark because of what question was to be asked next.

"Was this reported to the police?" Grant asked.

Alan shrugged. "No idea. A passing fishing boat brought him in. Another crabbing boat that berths in Flushing."

"Thank you, Alan," Grant said. "I've got your number; I'll call if I need anything else."

Alan took his cue and nodded. "Pleasure," he said and walked back the way they had come.

"What are you thinking?" DS Clark asked.

"What are *you* thinking, sergeant?"

"I thought I said call me Lucy," she said.

"Okay, Lucy. What are you thinking?"

"I think it's a possibility that John Trevithick recognised the people, or at least one of the people digging up the grave."

Grant nodded. "I think it's more like one of them recognised *him* and couldn't take the chance that Trevithick hadn't recognised them."

"We definitely think Trevithick's death is related though," she said flatly.

"We do."

"We need to look into his death then. I'd heard a man had drowned, a fisherman. But it was a snippet on the late-night local news. No *real* story. It happens quite a lot down here."

"It's not the only thing though."

"What else is there?"

Grant looked down at the grave, the fresh earth, the new flowers and the undamaged headstone. "We don't know for sure if the men digging were actually digging up a grave," he paused. "Or whether they were filling an *empty* grave back in."

Chapter Fifteen

"What do we do next?" DS Clark asked as Grant parked and switched off the engine.

The harbourmaster's office was directly ahead of them. They did not have an appointment, but Grant figured there would be someone around who could point them in the right direction. He tapped the steering wheel with his fingers, nibbled the inside of his cheek. It was anxiety, and it came on when he needed a drink.

Sixty-days...

The cruel irony was that he didn't miss the taste of it. But needed it instead to quell a host of emotions and irregularities within him - from breathing, to thinking, even to his equilibrium. It was as if the alcohol diluted something, balanced him out. Like the fuel to air mixture of an engine's carburettor. He knew when he felt like this, he would function better, in the short-term, with a drink. However, he also knew it merely greased a dangerous slope, that if stepped on, would not halt his descent until he reached rock bottom.

"Did you hear me, Grant?" she prompted.

"Sorry," he said. "Just thinking."

"What do we do next?"

"Let's see what happens here first."

"But the grave," she said. "What if you're right? What if they got to the bodies and were in fact filling the grave back in?"

"That's not the immediate question."

"What?"

"There's a bigger question."

She frowned. "What could be a bigger question than: *are the bodies still in the grave?*" "We know that there's probably a fifty-fifty chance they're not."

"Really?" She leaned back in her seat, the sun bright across her face. "I'd say there's a bigger chance they are still in the grave. It's a lot of work to dig out six bodies, take them elsewhere, presumably to a vehicle, then refill the plots."

"But they didn't finish refilling, if they started at all."

"What's the bigger question, then?"

He looked at her intently. "Why?" he said. "Why would they dig, or attempt to dig them up?"

"Anti-Islamic fuck-wits. Maybe they don't need a reason."

"Oh, they need a reason. And I think the reason is because they were buried. Most people are cremated these days. But Muslims request burial, and they need it within twenty-four hours. Now, the Hafeez family didn't make this, unfortunately. But the Islamic community stepped in and paid for the plot and sought to get the ceremony performed and had them buried soon after. Now, they were found drowned, and the cause of death confirmed this. I have seen the post-mortem, and I have to say for a family washed up on the beach with the wreckage of their boat and the whole sorry immigrant crisis story around them, as well as pressure from the Islamic community to get them in the ground ASAP, possibly with a little departmental influence to avoid an ethnic or racial situation, then I suppose the coroner's report is about right," he paused. "But there was no indication of foul play. So, the bodies were released to the Islamic charity that paid for the family plot, and that should have been an end to it."

"So, why do you think someone wanted them..." She searched for the words but shrugged lamely. "...dug up?"

"I think my boss made a few enquiries and spooked someone. Someone who is in the know, on the inside. He wasn't happy with something, and other than staying for a period of illness and recovery in his family holiday home at the point, I don't know what else would have prompted him to look into it."

"He's ill?"

Grant thought of Maitland, the man's death still raw. Thirty-six hours. Grant cursed inwardly at his date with Mary Hocking and missing the first time and date in the calendar. He had wasted precious time. The thought of the teddy bear DS Clark had found made him want to retch. Had he started to investigate sooner, could he have stopped what he assumed to be a movement of people? "Not anymore..." he conceded and added, "I think the Hafeez family were murdered. And I think whoever did it was convinced that their deaths would look to all the world like misadventure, and they would be cremated. The line of evidence would be severed totally. Now, when the commander of Special Branch has an inkling and starts a private inquiry, it causes a panic because somebody in the know hears of it. That prompts them to get the bodies before there is a chance of official exhumation and a thorough, detailed autopsy from the inside out."

"And poor John Trevithick recognised one or more of them?"

"No. I think *they* recognised John Trevithick and weren't sure if he had recognised them, so they killed him before he could talk. Or at least work it out."

"You think they drowned him?" she asked. "Made it look like an accident?"

"Fits the MO of the Hafeez family."

"Jesus..." she shook her head.

Grant opened his door. "Come on," he said. "Let's see if the harbourmaster can shed any light on it."

It was actually called the Falmouth Harbour Commissioner's Office. And the man in charge was Josh Gwennap. Judging from his movements, his physique and eyes, Grant put him in his forties, but his face was as weathered and as tanned as a crocodile's back. He sported a neatly trimmed greying beard and was wearing an inflatable life-vest, though uninflated, and wore a two-way radio on a strap across his vest. He also wore a fisherman's knife and a multi-tool in a pouch on his belt.

"I dealt with it personally," he said in reply to Grant's question regarding John Trevithick's death.

"You discovered the body?"

Gwennap shook his head. "Not like that," he said, his Cornish accent as broad as his shoulders. "I answered the distress call, met the boat on its way back in."

"The boat that found him?"

"Yes. I set aside an area on the quay, called the ambulance, but they weren't needed by the time they brought him in."

"He was alive when they found him?"

"Don't think so, but you always call an ambulance as a matter of course."

Grant nodded. "And the body went to...?"

"Treliske Hospital," he said. "Or the Royal Cornwall Hospital as it's known now, but nobody local uses anything else but the original name. There wasn't an inquest. Trevithick was seventy-years old and fell overboard pulling in his crab pots. It's dangerous work. The man had got himself caught up with the rope. I imagine he gulped a breath in panic and that's all it takes to start drowning."

"That's it? No coroner, no post-mortem?"

Gwenapp shrugged. "He was a fisherman. Even in summer, once you're a mile or so offshore the water is freezing cold. He's wearing jeans and wellington boots, a jacket and no life vest. He was seventy and like most fishermen, he wasn't much of a swimmer. You take's your chances, I'm afraid."

"Is he buried around here? Swanvale perhaps?" Grant cursed not asking Alan while he was up there.

"No, a cremation at Penmount Crematorium," he said. "Up the other side of Truro. Small service. I attended, I didn't really know him, but you know..." he shrugged.

Grant did know. He had attended more than a few services for people he did not know but had been a part of the investigation into their death. He had gone to a few to watch the crowd as well. Killers loved to go to their victim's funeral.

"Who found the body?" DS Clark asked.

Gwenapp turned to her. "Local chap. Does a bit of potting and long-lining. Not regular, like. He used to but now works as a handyman and gamekeeper nearby. Over at

Trenvarth Manor. He keeps a boat in Flushing too. Knew John Trevithick well."

"What's his name?" Grant asked, a tingle running up his spine. He already knew the answer.

"Bunt. Pete Bunt," the harbourmaster said. "He was at the service, too."

Chapter Sixteen

"I've never signed an exhumation order before."

"Few police officers have."

"But why don't *you* want to do it?"

"I don't want it to be blocked."

"Who is going to do that?"

"Someone might," Grant paused. "There is a *someone* working against justice here, somebody with an ear to the ground and an eye on the law."

"Who do you suspect?"

"Well, we need to find out who visited the Swanvale graveyard because clearly more action could have been taken."

"That shouldn't be too difficult, it will all be logged on the PNC," DS Clark commented. She watched the road ahead and said, "Next left."

Grant slowed and took the left off the mini roundabout. They had driven on the Falmouth bypass and were heading back towards Camborne police station. He needed to log into the police database and make some checks. He also needed a good internet connection to search for a few things. He wanted DS Clark to see to exhuming the bodies, or simply confirming that they were still in the ground. If they were, then he wanted a Home Office pathologist to perform an in-depth autopsy on the Syrian family. That was not as easy as it sounded. He was hoping that a detective sergeant would have enough clout to set the ball rolling. But he didn't know Cornwall and its procedure. And he didn't want to make the case high-profile. He had instructed DS Clark to over-play an obvious race card from the start. A dead family deserved justice. Would an exhumation not be granted quicker if the family were white? That sort of thing. Exhumation is a sacrilegious act in Islam, so perhaps it should be done quietly and without unnecessary obstruction or procedure. If this was to be refused, was it a race thing? Nine out of ten times people wouldn't want to be involved in questions like that. They would be susceptible to bending with the pressure.

"You need to play it," Grant said. "And you need to make it clear that the damage done to their grave indicated potential, or actual body snatching and that we are not certain whether or not this has been achieved."

"I'll get it done," she said.

Grant found himself driving through Lanner and onwards down into Redruth. Strangely, with the sun on it and a blue sky, it looked a little less grey and depressing. He commented on this to DS Clark.

"It's all granite around here. And Carn Brea, the big hill and monument over there," she said pointing to a hill which must have been just short of a mountain, "Seems to suck in the cloud and make it all grey and damp. To be fair, it's never usually bright and sunny like this around here."

"Well, it's a *little* less depressing than it was this morning," he commented flatly.

It was cloudy and grey in Camborne. But this was Cornwall, and the weather was different every few miles you travelled. Grant had read that it was something to do with being a narrow peninsular meeting the weather patterns from the Atlantic. The Gulfstream current warmed the water, and the Airstream was meant to sweep in and blow north of Cornwall. In recent years, the Airstream had shifted and that had left Cornwall with cooler, wetter summers. As if a place with such unsettled weather needed worse summers. Grant couldn't complain though, he hadn't seen rain for his entire stay, and the early evenings always seemed sunny and mild regardless of cloud or breeze in the daytime.

He parked the Alfa Romeo in a narrow space and squeezed out of his half-open door. The door creaked and Grant frowned. It hadn't been the most reliable vehicle he'd ever owned, but it felt good on the open road, and he enjoyed the tone of the exhaust. He made a mental note to get some WD40 the next time he stopped for petrol but doubted he would remember. Then he remembered that he needed to check the oil. Again. He saw DCI Warleggan getting into an unmarked Ford Focus at the other end of the carpark. Grant raised a hand, not to greet him but to indicate that he wanted to speak to him, but the car shot out of the carpark and turned left.

"I don't think he wanted to speak to you," DS Clark said sardonically.

"You don't say," Grant replied.

DS Clark led the way and opened the door with a swipe card and a four-digit code. "You'll need one of these," she said. "I'll speak to the duty officer and set you up."

"Thanks."

"So, I'll call the coroner and get something in progress

before knocking off," she said. "Unless there's anything else?"

"No, that's fine. Do I need anything to log on?"

"Yes. I'll sort you out with the password." She led the way through to the CID suite and the ginger-haired detective with the greying beard looked up as they entered. He said nothing, turned back to his screen. She leaned over a desk in front of Grant and tapped on the keyboard. "That should be okay. Unless you want to take the boss's office?"

Grant shook his head. "This'll do," he said. He felt he had made his point earlier. "When you get my pass card and give me the passcode, ask the duty officer to arrange an office for me with a computer terminal. I'll be back in for eight-thirty tomorrow morning, there must be a space somewhere they can shoe-horn me in."

She looked a little surprised but nodded. "I'll get onto it now, Grant," she said, then glanced at the detective who had looked up. "I mean, *Superintendent.*"

"Great," he said and sat down at the desk. He didn't look back up and she left to talk to the desk officer. He looked up when she was outside the suite. "Detective," he said.

"Yes, sir. Detective Sergeant Jago," he said. "Chris Jago."

"DS Jago, do you know where DCI Warleggan has gone? Or when he is planning on getting back?"

"I think he's knocking off duty, sir."

He won't be back, thought Grant. *Still licking his wounds...*

Grant checked his watch. It was an Omega Seamaster and was precious to him. He had won it in his final year of university in an international water polo match sponsored by the watch maker. The entire winning team had been awarded one. Most of the team had gone on to play in the Beijing and London Olympics, but Grant's drinking had ended any chance of that. He had pawned the watch once to pay for booze and rent, a rock bottom moment, and he was lucky enough to have managed to buy it back when he had reached fifty days' sobriety. Each time he looked at it, he knew he could make it. And this time, he would. He was sure he would...

The time was five-fifteen. It wasn't an unreasonable time to punch out, it depended upon what investigation was in progress. He knew that Warleggan would have put in more than a few twenty-hour shifts in his time, he wouldn't have made DCI if he hadn't, but he suspected that DCI Warleggan had merely wanted to make himself scarce. He couldn't blame the man, but he had more than a few questions for him when he returned to the station.

"Right, all done," DS Clark said, walking in with a file. "You'll have the broom cupboard next door." She smiled. "Joke. There's an interview room that's going to get a makeover in the next hour or so. Should be serviceable by the time you come in tomorrow."

"Great," Grant smiled. "Did you catch the coroner?"

"I did. He's going to be working until six, but he said he'd check his emails at home every hour or so until about ten. So, he'll evaluate the report and email me back."

"Was he... open to the request?"

"I think so. He agreed we need to know whether they are still in the ground or not. That's a given. It should be signed by the morning. He didn't hint as to whether we'd get the autopsy if they were still there, we need to ascertain that first. He agreed we don't want to have to fill it in after checking the graves, merely to dig them all out again, but he wanted to get a second opinion on it first and would forward our report on. I explained our findings and our doubt as to any conclusion of misadventure." She looked up as DS Jago walked past them without a word, she frowned at his apparent rudeness. From the way he was putting on his jacket, it was clear he was leaving his shift. "Sorry, where was I? Oh, yes... First, we get confirmation, but it would be worth calling him as soon as we discover whether or not they are there." She shivered. "Creepy, isn't it? I mean, laid to rest and then some monster digs you up, for Lord only knows what purpose..."

Grant had his theories, but he didn't share them with her. Better to wait and see if there would be an in-depth autopsy first. "Well, get our findings and theories down and email him as soon as you've finished."

"Okay," she said and went over to her workstation. She pulled out her chair and sat down heavily.

Grant logged onto the computer and made the searches he required on the police database. He opened the browser and started to search the internet, then flicked between the open tabs. He jotted on a notepad and occasionally saved documents or internet URLs to his personal cloud. He would be able to access them later from his laptop. He worked solidly for forty-minutes, then looked up as DS Clark stood up and pushed her chair under the desk.

"I'm done," she said.

"You sent it?"

"I have," she replied. "Do you want to see what I've sent?"

He wasn't one to micro-manage. She was an experienced detective sergeant. "No," he said. "I'll see you back here in the morning. I'm interviewing Mary Hocking about the assault at nine-thirty." He noted she looked disinterested. "Leave tomorrow free, you can assist me again."

"Really?" she smiled.

"Yes."

"Alright," she said, a little coyly. "I'll see you in the morning."

Grant returned to his screen and worked for another thirty-minutes and was satisfied that the CID suite would not be in use for the rest of the day. He shut down his computer and glanced down the corridor before heading to search DCI Warleggan's office.

Chapter Seventeen

G rant dropped the keys onto the kitchen worktop and opened the fridge. It was more than evident that he needed a shop. He knew that the fridge was going to be empty, but it was a force of habit to open it in hopeful anticipation. If he was going to be staying longer than he had initially anticipated, then he would need to get some supplies. There were two bottles of wine at the back of the fridge. They were screw top sauvignon blanc. Next to them were half a dozen European mini bottles of beer which he suspected to be from the Czech Republic, along with the four-pack that Mary had brought along last night. The alcohol was like a spectre. Present, foreboding and inevitable. He closed the door and picked up the kettle. Maitland had a fancy Italian coffee machine installed into a recess in the wall, but Grant had tried and failed to get it working. He filled the kettle, put it back on its base and took a sachet of coffee and a cafetiere out of the cupboard. He looked back at the kettle, then opened the fridge again. The beer and the wine were still there. He had resisted temptation before. He had dramatically poured all the alcohol down the sink in an act of finality, back when his wife had failed to support him and continued to buy it for herself and entertaining their friends, who had later all become *her* friends. But he knew that the act of ridding himself of the alcohol was one thing and the simplicity of driving to a supermarket or a local convenience shop was quite another. Whether he got rid of the drink or let it remain in the fridge calling to him didn't really matter. There was always easy access and he needed to overcome the urge. He took out his wallet and slipped out the photograph of his daughter Chloe. The photograph was creased and worn, it had been unfolded and looked at daily. She was laughing, sitting on a pony at a petting farm. Grant stood one side, and the photo had been folded, in a darker time, to hide his wife, who was standing on the other side. A snapshot of a happy family, unaware of the torment and misery, the disappointment and rawness of the split that lay ahead of them. He looked at the woman in the photograph, now his ex-wife. She had once been pretty and kind, but he had taken all of that away, eroded it to a husk. She would never love him again, and nor did he feel he deserved her love for that matter. In his darker hours, he would blame her for not giving him her support, for not accepting his alcoholism as an illness and fighting it alongside him as one would with something more tangible like a cancer, but ultimately, he knew the fight was always his and his alone. He had put too much weight on her, and more besides. She had played her part too, but his condition would always have been the catalyst. He still wasn't ready to unfold her, probably never would, but he would never tear the photograph and remove her presence altogether. She needed to be there as a permanent reminder, a symbol of consequence. Because without regret, there would never be hope or fulfilment.

The kettle switched off, seemingly boiling faster because of the distraction, and he made the coffee, poured it into an oversized mug and walked through to the lounge. The sun was low, almost touching the hill far beyond the creek and casting a golden hue on the water's surface. The tide was full and with little wind, the water looked like a mirror.

He drank a good mouthful of coffee and placed the cup down on the top of the bookcase, before opening the sliding glass doors. He took off his clothes, keeping his boxer shorts on. His heartrate quickened, there was an underlying panic he did his best to quell, but he knew he needed to do it, and he had already proved he was no oarsman in the rowing boat with DS Clark earlier.

Grant stepped out onto the grass, soft and warm underfoot. He walked the length of the garden and looked at the surface of the water, saw the depth of the mud and stones underneath. He estimated it was a little less than a metre. He looked each way, to the neighbouring property on his right, and to the grass-topped granite quay and area of grass to his left. There was nobody on the footpath, nobody anywhere in sight. He closed his eyes, saw the face in his dreams, the face of his nightmares. The water was no longer the same for him, but he must try to suppress his anxiety. He had been brilliant once. A phenomenal swimmer and diver, and fantastic at water polo. He felt a little less anxious and knew that it was now or never. His last time in the water had left him with nightmares, it was time to move on.

Grant leaped and shallow dived into the water. His chest and stomach scraped the bottom and sent up a great cloud of silt. He chanced opening his eyes and saw several flat fish darting off in front of him. The water was cool, but not unpleasant and he stroked hard, crawling and alternating his intake of breath under each arm, blowing a clear stream of bubbles with his head straight for three strokes. He could no longer see the bottom; the visibility was only around three feet or so and he was already out of his depth. He looked straight ahead, his eyes stinging from the salt, and kept his focus on the jetty. He was halfway across, and the current was negligible. He figured it was just about on high tide.

As he approached the jetty, he could see more, and the water was deeper. He was not entirely sure why the visibility was better here, but when he finally reached the jetty, he took a breath and dropped down, pushing his feet towards the bottom. The water was noticeably colder, and he estimated it to be around ten feet in depth.

Grant pulled himself out of the water and sat for a moment on the jetty. The sun was still visible, the rays warming him, but as he got up and walked to the path, the shade was cold and unforgiving. The ground was slippery under his bare feet, but he shortened his stride and made good progress. He was soon in the place where both he and DS Clark had been shot at. The place where she had found the teddy bear.

Now starting to shiver, Grant entered the wooded area. There was movement around him, scuffling and digging and the sound of birds darting through the undergrowth. His presence did not seem to scare them away. The ground ahead of him rose and there were granite boulders of varying sizes from football-sized fragments through to the size of family hatchbacks. After a few more paces, he realised that this must have been the distance and area from which Claude Roebuck had taken his two shots at them. He turned around and surveyed the area he had come from. Even without the rifle scope, he was convinced that

Roebuck would have been able to see that they were people and not deer. So why would Roebuck have risked shooting? Grant walked back the way he had come and stepped back onto the path. He continued the route that both he and DS Clark would have taken. The huge slabs of granite piled up on both sides, funnelling the pathway and then the area opened out into a clearing. At the far end of the clearing, he could see a gap in the granite. As he walked closer, he could see that it was a cave entrance. The light was fading fast, and with it the temperature had plummeted. Standing in only the pair of damp, white boxer shorts, Grant was cold and felt vulnerable. He glanced around him, then stepped into the cave entrance. It was pitch black, but just a few feet inside, he could see the heavy metal bars of a pair of double wrought iron gates. He caught hold of them and gave the structure a shake. It was solid but rattled in the middle. Feeling along he found that there was a half-inch gap where the two sections of bars met. A large padlock, as big as his fist shackled two rings, fastening them in place. He ran his hands over the edges nearest the stone wall and could feel enormous hinges set at three intervals.

Grant stood back. He had heard of such smuggling tunnels. There was even a black and white picture and short paragraph framed on the wall of the local pub across the water on the point. Used in the late seventeen-hundreds and early eighteen-hundreds by smugglers and wreckers to hide their bounty, there had been several discovered over the years. Grant assumed that Trenvarth Manor had such a concession going on two-hundred years ago. The rum and tobacco would have been brought in by boat coinciding with the appropriate tides and cover of darkness, perhaps even with the right amount of moonlight, and the contraband would be divvied up and walked out of the doors of the manor house and onto horse and carts for distribution across Cornwall, maybe even to London where it could buy influence. There was a reason that the owners of manor houses were rich back then. Things hadn't changed over the years, but it was the thought of what may be being smuggled that left Grant cold, and not just because of the night-time air. He looked down at the ground in the cave entrance. It was worn enough to have had multiple people passing through its entrance for a while.

There was nothing more he could do here, so he made his way back down the pathway, stopping occasionally when he heard movement in the undergrowth. Paranoia was getting the better of him and he was relieved when he reached the jetty. It was almost completely dark now, save for the golden strip of sunset above the distant hill at the far end of the valley. To his right, down the creek and towards the sea, it was dark as pitch, and he could see the lights of houses all along the point in the distance. He looked across the water, but could not see the Hemingway House, as he had forgotten to leave a light on. He cursed his lack of thought. But for his money, it was a direct swim straight out from the jetty. He closed his eyes, already seeing the face and the vision he so often felt recently when he looked at water.

It's all in the past, all in your mind...

He dived off the edge of the jetty and stroked powerfully out into the creek. He breathed to his right, every six strokes, a technique he used for powerful bursts to put on a good speed and distance. He didn't hesitate, merely kept up the pace. After a dozen or so breaths, he glanced up and realised that he was way off course. He had drifted a long way down river, and he panicked for a moment as he treaded water and searched for the house. It was a hundred-metres further up-river and he changed course and swam as hard as he could. After several minutes of ploughing onwards, he raised his head to find he had made no progress whatsoever, and he felt a rush of fear within him, his heart-beat beating from both the exertion and panic. He aimed for the bank now and started to breaststroke, as his breathing was off, and he was too tired to front-crawl. For the first time since the incident in London, the wounded muscle in both his shoulder and torso gave him pain, akin to sharp bursts like cramp. He made a little progress, but Loe Creek was passing by, and he was heading down river rapidly. At the quay, the creek veered right sharply, and it was open water all the way out into the Carrick Roads. Panic was with him now, and he started to snatch his breath. For the first time in his life, he was genuinely fearful that he would drown. He took a huge breath, dipped his head and made a last surge for the bank. After perhaps thirty strokes, he raised his head and saw a figure running in pace with him on the footpath. Part of his subconscious mind marvelled on the speed in which he was being pulled out to sea. A more useful part of his mind saw the life ring the person threw and thankfully, realised they had thrown it well down river from him. He breast-stroked hard, watching the life ring bob on the surface, then pull tightly on its orange buoy line. He snatched at it and missed. It was at the end of the length of rope and his heart sunk as he realised that there would not be another shot at this, but he kicked and stroked hard and finally caught hold, gripping for dear life. He continued to kick, felt the rope stretch and then felt himself stop dead in the current, which now pulled at him harder, putting a great deal of tension on the rope. He prayed they could pull him in, but he aided the effort by clutching the ring close and using his left hand to stroke as he kicked wildly with both legs. He could see the bank getting closer and after a dozen strokes and twenty metres or so, he felt the bottom with tired feet. He righted himself, and waded against the current, feeling the tautness of the rope anchoring him upright and bringing him steadily in.

As he reached the bank he collapsed, exhausted. His legs were still in the water, and he felt the current wash over his skin. He struggled upwards and rolled over onto his back, heaving for breath and a warm rush of euphoria enveloping him like a warm blanket. After a full minute, he looked up at the person who had undoubtedly saved him.

"Jesus, Grant," Mary Hocking said. "You were doing well up until you hit the middle of the creek. But that's where the river is running permanently, whether the tide's coming in, dropping or slack. Combine it with a falling tide and boats with fair sized engines struggle to cross in a straight line." She smiled, a thick lock of red hair slipped down across her face, and she swiped it aside and tucked it behind her ear. "You're like most emmets," she said. "You could swim all day long in a pool, but you don't know shit about the tides and *real* swimming..."

Chapter Eighteen

Grant wasn't quite walking wounded, but he was able to lean on Mary as she walked with him along the riverbank, without feeling that he was acting unduly dramatic. She was warm and he could feel the heat coming off her. He was shivering uncontrollably by the time they reached the garden and walked through the welcoming doors of the house.

Mary closed the glass doors and drew the curtains. She took a throw off the leather sofa and wrapped it around him. "Hot shower for you," she said. "You're bordering on hypothermic."

He would have agreed, had his teeth not been chattering so much, she put an arm around him and guided him up the stairs and into the bathroom. The shower was a double cubicle and had three jets, one large ceiling rose and two more from the sides. The water was heated by a gas combi-boiler, and the heat was instant, and the water pressure was phenomenal. Grant stepped in and the water burned and stung like pins and needles. Mary placed a towel on the heated towel rail for him.

"Thank you," he stammered slightly. He couldn't imagine getting out of the water alive once he had drifted past the point. He would surely have drowned. He looked at her sheepishly. "I think you just saved my life," he admitted meekly.

She smiled, leaned into the shower and kissed him on the cheek, her hair getting wet with spray. He knew what she had done for money earlier that day, what that made her, but there was an innocence in her eyes, and an infectiousness to her manner that made him look past it all. "You're welcome," she said. "Perhaps you can save mine in return..." She didn't smile or add *someday* to the sentence as banter. She said it seriously, and he looked back at her with concern.

"Mary..."

She cut him off before he could continue. "Coffee!" she said. "I'll get some on. You need to warm from the inside, too." She hovered at the door. "I can get another Chinese delivery, if you want to try again. We've got the life-threatening situation out of the way first tonight. What can go wrong?" She didn't give him the chance to answer and closed the door after her.

Grant felt his core warming. The water had been tolerable, but he knew it was the shock and exertion that had knocked it out of him. The hot coffee would help, and he was ravenous now that Mary had mentioned food. He could almost taste and smell the aroma of a Chinese takeaway and had forgotten all about the wine and beer in the fridge.

He switched off the cascades of hot water and stepped carefully out onto the tiled floor. The window and mirrors had steamed like a sauna, and he could barely see across the room to the door. He rubbed the condensation away from the cabinet mirror and looked at himself. He had been convinced that he was going to die. He had felt the same way twice before in his life and for some reason staring at himself in the mirror was a comfort. As if it were a chance to both condemn and praise himself, celebrate his evasion of the alternative to what he was seeing now. His reflection was confirmation of his survival.

Grant dressed in the master bedroom. Jeans and a sweatshirt. He was warmed through, and now he just wanted to slouch. He couldn't remember feeling so exhausted. He thought about Mary and how he had seen her earlier today. Dressed for a performance. Now she was the girl next door, in jeans and a tight-fitting T-shirt, a cardigan over her shoulders. She had run quickly down the quay and the footpath along the riverbank. He hadn't noticed her footwear, but suspected she wore trainers. So different from when he had seen her in the leather dress that had barely covered her dignity and the ridiculous heels which had brought her up to his own height. But it had all seemed part of an act. She hadn't been comfortable, and Grant sensed that this was the real Mary Hocking and he wanted to know more about her and the choices she had made in life.

As he walked down the staircase, he could hear Mary in the kitchen. She was preparing something, the sound of the microwave and the fan oven, of the cutlery drawer opening. Grant knew he did not have any food in the house and thought that mentioning another takeaway was more of a joke than a possibility. Perhaps she had brought some food with her or had stopped by after shopping for some and decided to share. He was famished after the swim, needed to eat and wasn't about to put up an argument.

"Sorry to have interrupted, but I think I might have

saved you again," DS Clark said, reaching two plates out of the cupboard.

Grant recoiled when he saw her, then gradually regained some composure. "Where's Mary?" he managed to say, almost casually.

"I sent her packing," she said. "Mind you, perhaps I was too late?" She laughed as she opened a microwave ready meal and started to spoon rice and chicken korma onto both plates. "I mean, she had wet hair, and you've just got out of the shower. Mate's rates? Or did she charge full whack? What is that by the way? Must be at least fifty-quid for a ginger..."

Grant glared. "It wasn't like that," he protested. He watched her spoon something red on the plate, tikka he thought. It smelled good. "She *saved* me, actually."

"From what, a night of abstinence?"

"From drowning."

"Seriously? I thought you were a good swimmer, you know, from what they said in the papers..." she trailed off.

Grant walked over and picked up some naan bread. It was steaming. He dipped it in the red sauce and took a bite. "I swam over and took a look at the ground on Trenvarth Estate."

"What? Grant, they shot at us last time!"

"I swam over, and it was okay. On the way back I hit a bad current and missed the bank. To be more accurate, I missed Loe Creek entirely and nearly missed the point altogether. If Mary hadn't thrown me a line, I think I would have gone right on out to sea..."

"Jesus..." she said but wasn't compelled enough to stop dishing up the meal.

"What did you say to her?" he asked. He owed Mary

more than the short shrift from a colleague he had only known for twenty-four hours.

"I just told her to go." She shrugged. "Look, Grant, I don't know what you've got going on with her. But I'm surprised you'd have *anything* to do with her after finding out what she does for a living today. But if you don't mind that, then I'll butt out. We'll forget all about our drink or whatever after this. But she's bad news. She falls in and out of love with the wrong people, she's a train wreck socially, financially, in every conceivable way."

Grant nodded. "She saved me tonight. And she said I might be able to *save* her. I've seen a lot of women do what she does, but I have never met one who should do it less. There's something not right about why she does it. But regardless of that, she genuinely saved my life tonight. I owe her, and that's reason enough for you to *butt out*, as you say."

"Fine. Fill your boots." She snatched up her handbag and made for the door. Grant had seen this before. He'd seen it in every relationship he'd ever had. Maybe it was him. She would stop and have the last word before she left. And the last word was always the most cutting. "I just hope you have enough money to pay for what I might have given for free..." She was genuinely tearful as she wrenched open the door and slammed it behind her.

Grant picked up a plate and a fork and started to eat. DS Lucy Clark's words were nothing to him. He had liked her, fallen a little bit for her in a day, but she had shown him something more to her character. He didn't believe that her bad feeling towards Mary Hocking was down to the fact the woman had sold sex. There had to be more. Grant had fallen out of his little crush in less time than it had taken to dish up a chicken tikka. But what worried him most was that she had not asked anything about what he had done, or what he had discovered on the Trenvarth Estate. She had concentrated only on Mary. There was so much more to her dislike of her, but right now, he was too tired and hungry to think.

Chapter Nineteen

The office that had been made for him was a windowless and oppressive box. There was a computer and monitor rigged up with access to the mainframe, server and PNC or Police National Computer database. He had a telephone and a printer. Someone had even left a few pens, pencils and a notepad on the desk.

"We've got our exhumation," DS Clark said, hovering in the doorway, her body wrapped around the doorframe. She did not show any animosity from last night. No emotion whatsoever. It could have been better, but it could have been a whole lot worse.

"You surprise me," said Grant coolly. "That was pretty straightforward."

"Well, you said to play the race card. Nobody likes a scandal."

"Indeed."

"If the bodies are still there, then we have to call for the full exhumation. This will be a fact-finding-operation, if you will."

"Well, can you get whoever does the digging thing sorted for asap? I want to be on this today."

"A team of forensics officers, I suppose. I'll try them first. I've never been involved with anything like this."

"Well start now."

"I'll call the Swanvale numbers as well, tell them to expect us today."

He nodded. "Good. Are you okay?" he asked.

"Sure, *Superintendent*, why do you ask?"

Grant thought for a moment, decided to leave it at that. "As you were, DS Clark. Can you get a minion to make me a coffee please?"

She nodded and left. He looked at the four walls and stood up decisively. He was isolated here, needed to see what was going on. The CID suite was three doors down and fifty feet away. DCI Warleggan was in his office. DS Clark was talking at the whiteboard with the overweight detective, DC Hastings. Two younger detectives were looking at a screen, one bent over the desk pointing at the screen, the other sat comfortably back in his chair. They looked up but said nothing as Grant walked in. They would have heard about yesterday. Half of the police in Cornwall would have heard about yesterday.

DCI Warleggan walked out from his office with DS Jago. "Good morning, *Acting* Superintendent," he said churlishly. "How would you like to tie up our criminal investigation department today? Another leisurely lunch? Some more swimming? I imagine just some crazy golf, a pasty and an ice cream and you will have ticked off your holiday list." Warleggan smiled, held up a hand. "Just a joke. Seriously, how can *my* CID team be of assistance?" His tone would have suggested it had been anything but a joke.

Grant returned his smile, although his eyes were humourless. "Thank you, DCI Warleggan. Your sarcasm is expected, although thoroughly unappreciated. But since you feel confident enough to attempt to humiliate me in front of your team, I will return the gesture. You can start by telling everybody here why you decided not to take further action when the Hafeez family's grave was desecrated?"

For a moment Grant thought the DCI was going to swing at him. Part of him hoped he would. He was ready and more than able. But the man looked crestfallen instead.

Warleggan shrugged, looked at DS Jago. "You went out to that shout, fill the *Acting* Superintendent in, will you?"

"No, I asked you. I was addressing *you*. I have seen DS Jago's report. It goes on to say that it looked like the grave had been dug up. That the vandalism was in fact superficial. Damage to a vase and some edging stones, but the headstone was intact. It was flagged as no further action. By *you*." Grant stared at Warleggan. "Care to explain?" DCI Warleggan looked flustered, but Grant didn't give him the opportunity to respond. "While we're at it, and we broached this subject yesterday in case you have already forgotten, why were the sea conditions not considered? Flat and calm, according to the Harbourmaster's report. Not the sort of conditions to sink an inflatable vessel which was equipped with ten separate air chambers. Then there's the matters which struck me as obvious. No engine, no equipment found, not even an oar. The tide brings in all six bodies, the remains of the boat, but no oars. Interesting. Or what we detectives would call *suspicious*. But we have the biggest anomaly of all, in that the boat was purchased just three miles from this station."

"It's a big ocean. Things go missing. But what you're

saying is that their deaths were in fact murder?" Warleggan scoffed. "Those illegal immigrants..."

"Asylum seekers!" Grant snapped. "Two doctors, both successful professionals, both trained in Europe, one of them educated at Oxford, and a further two adults and two innocent children. Their deaths are unexplained at best. They were not commodities or unfortunate statistics. They were killed in this country, whether or not it was an accident or misadventure, there were enough anomalies to have investigated further." He looked around at the rest of the team, exasperated. "Who else here thought that the incident required further action?"

The detectives looked blankly at each other. There were awkward expressions all round, until DC Hastings slowly raised his hand. "Sir, I pointed out that there were no oars, engine or fuel tanks," he said, avoiding the DCI's glare. "I just thought, well, you know... We're not near Dover, they couldn't have set out from France without an engine..."

"Good," Grant said. "And why was this not added to the report?"

The officer was almost shaking, his face flushed scarlet. He was sweating profusely. Grant knew the man's heart would be pumping wildly. "Sir, the DCI discounted it..."

Grant nodded, looked back at the officers in turn. Warleggan had turned pale. He noted that DS Clark was suppressing a smile. "Now, the man who disturbed the people digging the Hafeez family's grave, did it not seem a coincidence that he died later that day?"

There were looks all round, a few vacant expressions. DS Clark half raised a hand but lowered it sheepishly. "It does, on reflection. But the death was deemed an accident and it wouldn't have come across CID's desk."

"But it did," Grant corrected her.

She frowned. "But..."

"Sir," one of the men Grant had not seen before today held a hand up, just halfway then dropped it back to his side. He avoided looking at Warleggan. "DC Adams, sir. I mentioned that it was a coincidence that he died the day he witnessed the event at Swanvale. But I knew John Trevithick. I grew up as a harbour rat, always fishing and swimming, diving off the harbour wall. I *lived* my summers at Flushing. Trevithick was fishing all that time. I saw him swim with his nieces and nephews a few times, taught them where to jump off the quay. He wasn't a great swimmer technically, but he was better than most fishermen."

"It was flagged up. And yes, DC Adams queried events, but it was overruled, and no further action was taken." Grant looked at DCI Warleggan. "Why was that?"

DCI Warleggan shook his head. "The man was seventy. He went overboard, got caught up in his lines..." He paused. "Christ, it's not like we have the budget to deep dive into *everything*. Sometimes, accidents happen."

"The man *was* seventy, but he was as fit as a fiddle," Grant interrupted. "He dug graves, trimmed and tended the gardens of rest. He set and pulled up his lobster and crab pots most days. By hand. I suspect he was fitter than anybody in this room."

"But he couldn't swim," Warleggan protested.

"No? DC Adams told you different."

"The statement from his wife said he hadn't swum in years!"

"But that would indicate that he *could* swim, and you don't forget how to swim. It comes back pretty quickly if you fall over the side of a boat."

"I hear you weren't so familiar with swimming last

night," Warleggan scoffed. "We all know you can swim. Better than those you try to save, at least..."

"One more word!" Grant snapped. He stepped closer, just a pace separating the two men. "I dare you." He glanced sideways at DS Clark. "This come from you?"

"No!" she snapped, her face flashing with anger. "Of course not!"

"Take your lover's tiff outside," Warleggan goaded. "We've got next to no budget and too many cases on our books to waste any more time on this! But it came from your other woman. My, you work fast. Is that why your wife left you? Perhaps she couldn't keep up with your womanising?"

Grant clenched his fists by his side. It was all he could do to stop himself from hitting the man in front of him. He took a breath, felt the adrenalin subside a little. "I've tried with you," he said. "I was sent here to look into something, discover if there was more to it than what everyone else had taken on face value. But what I've discovered, and I know to be certain, is that you are largely ineffective. You have a high proportion of unsolved cases, far higher than the national average. You have two ongoing murder investigations that are going nowhere, four and six years in and still no one in the frame. Now, Devon and Cornwall Constabulary have the worse murder investigation success rate in the entire country. Blame part of that on the eleven million tourists each year, blame the geographical size of the region, blame the cutbacks. But today, for the Hafeez family's case, I blame *you* DCI Warleggan, and you alone. I have spoken to the Chief Constable at Middlemoor, and you are to go over to Bodmin today and join CID on clear-up duties until further notice. You of course have the right to speak with your police federation representative, but at this stage I would advise it as career and pension suicide. Simply slide in and offer your services, and when I am finished here, you can come back and work with the full respect of your former team," Grant paused, eyeing the people in front of him. "Or not, I suppose..." Warleggan lunged forwards in a rage, but Grant simply twisted sideways and Warleggan lost his balance and fell across a desk, knocking the computer monitor to the floor. The man struggled back to his feet and Grant turned to DS Jago and DC Adams. "It appears that DCI Warleggan is feeling faint. Please take him outside for some fresh air." He waited until the two men helped the sheepish looking DCI out of the office then said, "I'm going to interview a witness." He paused, looking at DS Clark, who looked back at him, her eyes wide from what she had just witnessed. "And get somebody onto that coffee."

Chapter Twenty

"I didn't think you'd show."

"I seem to remember you gave me little choice."

Grant looked at Mary Hocking as he handed her the cup of tea. She wasn't the woman he had seen at the rented house in the leather dress and the comedy high heels. This was her. Hair as red as a summer sunrise pulled back in a ponytail, no makeup, not that he could tell at least, and wearing a thin knit pullover and a pair of faded jeans. She was pretty but understated.

"Well, maybe after last night, things have changed," he said. "Thank you."

"You were doing all right," she said. "But you ended up fighting against the current. Sometimes you have to go with it."

"Is that just swimming or is it a metaphor for life?"

She sipped the tea from the paper cup and looked at him non-committedly. "It's a metaphor for survival."

"Your survival?"

She shook her head. "I'll not talk here, but I *do* want to talk."

"But you're here to talk."

"I'm here for a statement about the two men who beat you up."

Grant subconsciously touched his swollen, almost black eye socket. It was sore across his cheek and into his jaw. "You knew them, didn't you?"

"No."

"You're lying."

"Prove it."

"I intend to."

She shrugged. "Like I said, prove it."

"You know Pete Bunt, don't you? He works for Claude Roebuck on Trenvarth Estate, just across the water from where I'm staying." He watched her expression, there was a flicker in her eyes, nothing more. But she picked up the tea and sipped. She was buying time. "You know him, don't you, Mary." It wasn't a question now; it was a statement of fact. "He was the one with the shotgun."

"What happens when you get to the bottom of whatever hole it is you're digging?"

"Pardon?"

"You heard."

Mary's accent had dropped a little further down the Cornish scale. Grant continued to study her face, noticed she looked defiant, resolute. He wasn't going to hear what she didn't want to tell. Maybe it was her red hair, her emerald eyes, but he knew she could have a temper. Perhaps it was a cliché, but he had found redheads to have hidden depths you didn't always want to probe. And other depths that you did. He could see she was trying to keep calm. The cup of tea was on the table, her hands clenched together. "I'm based in London. I'll be going back and continuing my duties there."

"Exactly," she said. "And where will that leave me when you're gone?" She stood up. "I'll talk some more, but not here. I don't trust the police here."

"Certain officers?"

"What do you think?"

"Sit down, Mary."

She glared down at him. "Don't tell me what to do. Am I under arrest?"

Grant shook his head. "No, I..."

"Then open that bloody door and let me out!" she snapped. "You'll be gone from here soon, but I'll still have my shit life and have to carry on doing what I do! Now open the door and let me out!"

Grant had made more than one mistake. He had tried to keep the talk unofficial, and he had negated the use of a recording system. He had no other officer present and he had closed the door on a young and attractive woman and himself. She was shouting at him, and it would not go unnoticed in the offices outside. He felt flushed with anguish and adrenalin, but only by his own stupidity. He got out of his chair, tried to give her a wide berth for the door, but she was on him in a flash. She prodded him in the chest, her face just inches from his own.

"You don't know anything!" she screamed at him. "All you want is to come down here from the big smoke and show us how we're not as good as you, how you get things done..." She jabbed her finger in his chest again and he caught hold of her by the arms, pushed her away to arms-length. "You're hurting me!" she shouted.

The door opened and DS Clark stood in the doorway with DCI Warleggan. DC Hastings hovered behind them. Grant looked at them for a moment, then let go of Mary and stepped back a pace. "It's not what it looks..." he trailed off.

He'd heard it before, hadn't believed the words then, wouldn't if he were them either.

Warleggan glared as him. "Not content with assaulting me, you're hurting a witness now. What, trying to coax her into a false statement?" He stepped aside, ushered DS Clark and DC Hastings through. "Lucy, see that the young lady is escorted to interview room three safely. Constable, escort *Acting* Superintendent Grant out of here."

"It wasn't like that," said Mary. "I just got upset, is all."

"Come with me, please," DS Clark said impassively.

Mary looked back at Grant. Her expression was one of regret, but she wasn't making any more waves. She followed DS Clark out into the corridor.

DCI Warleggan turned to Grant. "I'll catch up with you later. I'm going to make some calls of my own. Don't go too far now. How dare you lay a finger on me in front of my team..."

"You took a swing at me," Grant replied. "I could have knocked your teeth out, but I chose to avoid you instead."

"You've made a big mistake."

"You're making a bigger one. I believe there has been a premeditated and determined attempt to shut the Hafeez case down, to make it less than it is. I have already made findings, that I will not share at this time. Not until the taint on Cornwall's CID is clear to me."

"What findings? More than the bollocks and supposition you've come up with so far, I hope."

"You'll find out when the time is right," Grant stared at him coldly.

DC Hastings placed his hand on Grant's shoulder. "This way, Sir..."

"Remove your hand or you won't be able to use it for a month." Grant continued to stare at DCI Warleggan. DC

Hastings released his grip and stepped back. He looked unsure, but it wasn't the man's fault. Grant relented, nodded towards the open door. "Go on then, DC Hastings, lead on..."

The detective led the way, but Grant veered away from him and walked past the CID suite. He followed the corridor with the detective calling after him, "Sir! Sir, you have to come with me..."

Grant stopped, waited for the man to catch up. "You made a call, Detective Constable. It was a good call. You looked at the evidence and drew a good conclusion. DCI Warleggan deemed it no further action. He still did that with Adams and his personal knowledge of the fact that John Trevithick could indeed swim. And he took DS Jago's report concerning the damage to the grave which looked more in common with grave robbing than mindless vandalism. There's a connecting factor here, and he seems to have persuaded Mary Hocking to refrain from making a complaint about the man who sexually assaulted her the night two men tied me up, held me at gunpoint and beat me up. This is bullshit policing, DC Hastings. *Don't* become a part of it."

The young man looked unsure, but Grant could see he had got through to him. "What do I..."

"You turn around and go back to your workload. DCI Warleggan wanted you to escort me out. He never mentioned detaining me. Go back to work," he said and headed for the exit.

Chapter Twenty-One

Mary Hocking walked out of the police station a full hour later. She exchanged words with DS Clark at the glass doors and walked down the ramp. She looked dejected at first, but her bounce was back in her step by the time she reached her Mini Cooper in the carpark. She swung her bag onto the passenger seat and slunk down into the driver's seat and closed the door.

Grant turned and ran back to his car. He had left the station and driven around Camborne's one-way system and parked up fifty metres before the building came into view. He then made his way further forward on foot, saw that her car was still parked and waited. Grant now started the Alfa Romeo – always a tentative time - and with relief as the engine purred into life, he eased forward, catching a glimpse of the tiny Mini as it accelerated away. He gunned the engine and sailed on past the police station, catching up with the Mini quickly, then dropping back to let another car out of a junction. He was comfortable with the lead she had on him and the car between them gave him essential cover. She was a swift driver and when the car in front turned off, he had to speed up to maintain a visual. The road was quiet with little traffic. He hoped he was not obvious, but he knew that most people ignored their mirrors in day-to-day driving. She had no reason to suspect that she was being followed, so he relaxed and settled in approximately three-hundred metres behind her.

After passing through woods and sweeping down a hill towards the sea, Grant saw that they had reached Portreath. There was a harbour to the right of the beach and an island just offshore to the left. The beach looked idyllic. Golden sand, crashing white surf fringing the dark blue ocean. They were on the north coast now, and the scenery was dramatic. Huge cliffs hemmed the beach on two sides, and the surf crashed at the base of the cliffs and surged upwards, casting its spray and colourful mini rainbows in the sunlight. Here, the sea worried the shoreline, cast its anger upon the rocks. Grant could see groups of surfers beyond the breakers, more making their way down the beach to the shoreline. He watched the Mini pull into the left and park on the newly tarmacked drive of an expensive-looking, and thoroughly modern property. Again, he saw that it was for let by Keith & Davey, the same company as the property Mary had been working from in Loe Creek.

Grant parked his car on the other side of the road. There were no lines and by the look of the vehicles with roof racks and stickers, surfers had parked here to avoid the fees in the carpark, which was clearly in view at the bottom of the road on the fenced edge of the beach. He could see Mary sitting in her car. She was talking on her mobile phone. Moments later, a red Range Rover Sport pulled in behind her. A thin, balding man got out. He had the features of a weasel. His eyes were close together, preda-tory. There was something unnerving about the way he moved, like he had excess nervous energy. He walked over to the Mini and took a set of keys out of his pocket and handed them to her through her open window. They talked for less than a minute, Mary nodding like she was receiving instructions. She got out of the car and walked to the house, disappearing down a set of steps. Grant realised that the house was built on a split level. He imagined the lounge being upstairs affording the best view of the ocean.

The man got back inside the Range Rover and reversed out onto the road. Grant got out of the car and took out his mobile, holding it to his ear as if in conversation. He nodded, then stepped up to the window of the vehicle, made an act of putting the person on the other end of the call on hold. The man looked surprised, but stopped the vehicle, nonetheless.

"Hi, sorry to trouble you," said Grant. "Is this your house?"

The man seemed to weigh him up for a moment. "No," he said. "My company is handling the rental. I'm Keith Davey," he paused as Grant held out a hand to shake. He responded in an alpha-male manner, looked disappointed in Grant's neutral handshake and moved on. "I'm the managing director of Keith and Davey, estate agents." Grant frowned at the sign. The man added, "It's just me, not a partnership. The partner thing added kudos, back when I needed it," he smiled. "I don't need that now. We're the largest letting agency in Cornwall."

"Wow," Grant said like he was impressed. He hoped his acting was up to it.

"So how can I help?"

Grant smiled. "I love this house. Is it likely to come up for sale?"

"I doubt it. It's up for a year-long let though." He looked

Grant up and down, glanced across at the Alfa Romeo. "We have plenty of other properties though. There's sure to be something in your price range."

Grant figured that from the look the man had given his clothes and the ten-year old Alpha Romeo with its battle scars from London traffic, he wasn't getting a year in a prime rental property over-looking the beach. He nodded and asked for a card. The man naturally had one to hand and handed it to him through the window. The glass was sliding up and the vehicle was backing out before Grant had put the card in his pocket. He walked back to his car across the road and got back inside to wait. He thought about the estate agent's handshake. He had learned a lot. You could tell much, if you kept your own neutral. There were limp-wristed affairs, overly powerful and unnecessary statements of strength, dominators who twisted the wrist to put their hand on top, and there were secret society methods, designed to welcome you to a club. Grant mused over Keith Davey's handshake as he waited in the car.

He did not have to wait too long. A car parked up in front of him and the man inside studied the house for a few minutes then took out his mobile phone and dialled. Grant noticed that the car was a family people carrier with children's sun blinds on the rear side windows. There were a family of stickmen in the rear windscreen. By the look of it the man had a nuclear family of a horse-riding wife and three children who enjoyed cycling, karate and tennis. He watched the man get out of the car, glance both ways and crossed the road to the house.

Grant got out and caught up with the man as he reached the driveway. "Sir, a word please." He held up his warrant card. "DI Grant," he said. It was easier to go with the rank that was printed on the card for all sorts of reasons.

Grant guided the shell-shocked man off the driveway and onto the grass verge. He could see simply from line of sight that they were out of view from Mary inside the house. The man was shaking. Grant would make it quick. "You're going into that house for sexual services, right?"

"No... I..." he stammered.

"Save it." Grant looked at the man. He was in his forties and losing condition. He could see the man's wedding ring. Maybe the man liked to play the odds, got a thrill out of the event, rather than just the sex. "Where did you find out about this?"

The man hesitated. "Am I under arrest?"

"That depends."

"On what?"

"On you answering my questions," Grant said curtly. "If I do arrest you, it will drag through court and your wife will find out."

"I'm just crossing the road," the man sneered. "You've got nothing on me." He went to turn around, but Grant pushed him hard against the hedge. "Hey!"

"Quiet. You contacted the woman in there by phone. I'm figuring once for the appointment, then another for directions when you were close, and a third time to let her know you had arrived. Right? Don't lie, the phone records will show, no matter what you do with your phone or sim card. I'm also guessing you found out about this on the internet. Your browser history will confirm as much. Your IP address will be logged." The man looked defeated. He nodded, found it hard to maintain eye contact. "Good," Grant said. "How much?"

"Two hundred."

"For what?"

"GFE..."

"What?" Grant asked. He'd spent the last ten years on counterterrorism. He would guess it showed.

"Girlfriend experience," the man said. "Like the sex you had with your girlfriend before she became your wife."

"What, cinema and fish and chips?" Grant laughed. "Okay, I'm guessing that's the works."

"It's everything. But it's mainly the kissing," the man explained. "Prostitutes don't normally kiss. It's sometimes difficult to get turned on without that. GFE is the *whole* package."

"Right," Grant nodded. He was learning on the job. "So, what website did you use?"

The man shrugged. "Just a generic search. Escorts, massage, Cornwall, GFE..."

"And she had a website?"

"Not her own, no. I went through a site called Punter Street in the end. You can enter what you're looking for, locations and description. She had photos on there. She looked nice."

Grant nodded. She would have looked good. He stared at the man. For what it was worth, he felt jealous. "Look, I'm going to give you some advice. You have a family and a wife. I've seen your stickmen in the window. The Pokémon sunshades." The man looked ashen, the colour draining from him. Grant guessed he had never been thinking of his kids prior to one of these assignations. "You're laying them down as chips in a game of roulette. Pretty soon, you'll bet everything precious to you on black and it's going to land on red. You get prosecuted for this sort of thing, well that's your marriage gone. That's your kids out of your life, because even if you have good access, do you think they'll want to be around the guy who threw his family in for sex with a prostitute? I'm figuring not. And it *will* come out. All sorts of shit you think you can keep covered up come out in a divorce." Grant had walked the walk. His addiction to alcohol had been the entire focus in his divorce, rightly or wrongly, he hadn't been painted in the best light. "That's the personal stuff. Now your job. A criminal record will change your employee contract. Your job will likely go. Sex offences never look good on a CV either, so that's the likelihood of another job gone too. A few months without salary and the rent or mortgage for the house you're no longer living in will dry up. That's without you missing the rent on whatever bolthole you've managed to rent. Now your credit has gone. You'll get in debt and the spiral will continue. Are you getting the picture?"

"Yes," he nodded. He seemed to be taking it in. The man's mobile phone rang. He had been holding it lamely in his hand. He glanced at the screen. "It's her," he said.

"Answer it. Tell her you'll be there in two minutes." Grant watched the man, noted the tone of his voice. He was guessing what fires of passion had burned within him as he parked the car had been extinguished by now.

"So, what do I do?" the man asked, putting the phone into his pocket. He looked shorter somehow. Defeated.

"You take that two-hundred quid, and you book a babysitter. You book a fancy restaurant, maybe even a hotel room. You stop being an idiot and spend some time with your wife. Do that once in a while, and hell, you won't even think about crap like this. And you won't risk losing it all again. You might even find she's been missing the best of you as well."

The man seemed to think on this. He nodded. "Okay," he said. "Can I go?"

Grant nodded and stepped up onto the driveway. He heard the man thank him, but he didn't look back. He followed the path round and stood by the solid oak door. He knocked twice, clear and loud.

He heard a bolt draw back and the handle turned. The door gave an inch, Grant saw there was no security chain, and he barged the door open with his shoulder. Mary gasped and stepped back. When she looked at him, her eyes blazed.

"What the hell are you doing?"

"Your appointment had a change of heart." He stepped inside and looked at her. She was wearing a figure-hugging red dress. Her hair was down, and Grant noticed blonde tresses among the red.

"What have you done?" she asked. "I need that client!"

"Client? Punter, surely."

He didn't see it coming, but she slapped him across the cheek, and he recoiled. His face was still sore from the beating, now it felt raw.

"You don't understand!"

"Then tell me!" He placed a hand on his cheek, but it made no difference to the pain.

"What have you done?" she said again. She kicked off the high heels and walked off into a large lounge with an entire wall of glass looking over the bay. "Oh no, I don't believe this..."

Grant followed her. "What's going on? Why won't you say who attacked me, who felt you up and dragged you out of the house?"

"For God's sake Grant! Let it go!" She flopped down on the leather sofa and cradled her head in her hands. "You've made some real trouble for me..."

"It's a couple of hundred quid," he said. "I'll square it."

"You'll square it? What if he talks? What if..."

"What?"

"Forget it."

"Tell me, Mary."

She looked up at him. "Why do you think I work nights on the bar at the pub?"

"For extra cash," he replied.

"Extra cash, yes. Or more simply, for *cash*. If I *wanted* to do this work, worked the hours and could keep the money, then I could earn three or four-thousand a week." She wiped tears from her eyes with her fingers and palms. "I earn minimum wage, for twenty-hours a week. I could make that with one half-hour appointment. But the money I earn at the bar is for me, and I'm damned if *my* money will ever come from *this*."

"Tell me what's going on."

"Just go," she said. "You've done enough, believe me."

"Who is making you do this?" Grant asked.

"What do you care?" She closed her eyes and tilted her head to the ceiling.

"Come with me," he said. He wasn't even sure what he meant, but he knew he hated seeing her like this. "I can help. I can keep you safe, help you get out of this."

"You can't *fix* me," she said, looking at him through glossy eyes, her mascara smudged. "I'm not a project. I'm a person and if you are offering to help me, you need to see it through."

"I'm a police officer," he said. "I can get you help and protection. If you are being forced into this, then you need to talk to me."

"I don't trust the police. Not down here. The people I'm involved with get away with too much for me to trust the police."

"Who are you saying is bent?"

She hesitated. "Do you mean it? You can help me?"

Grant nodded. "I'm getting a picture, but it's not very clear. Hazy, to say the least. Perhaps you can help fill in the gaps?"

"I can try," she said. "But I need to know you won't leave before it's sorted out."

"I won't let you down."

She looked down at her phone. It was vibrating on silent. She looked at the screen. "It's him," she said. "Will you help me if I tell you everything?"

He nodded. "Answer it," he replied. "And put it on speaker for me..."

Chapter Twenty-Two

Grant cursed the strength of his phone signal. He seemed to have done it hourly since he had arrived. He had driven down into the village of Portreath, turned around when he found a turning wide enough and taken the steep hill back out. He craned his neck as he passed the house and saw that Mary was getting into her Mini. He had promised to help, and she now seemed resolute. He was convinced she had turned her back on the sex trade.

Grant missed the left turning back towards Camborne, but he saw from the vehicle's satnav map that the coast road joined the A30 at Hayle, and he felt the drive would go a long way towards clearing his head. He kept glancing at the phone on the passenger seat, but there was still no service. He used the time to think. He wound the window down halfway and gunned the engine. The Alfa was a great car to drive through the twisting corners and he relished the exhaust note as he downshifted. He wasn't exactly speeding, but he wasn't setting a good example either. Before long, after a longish straight, where he caught a good view of the sea and St. Ives in the distance, he came to a series of bends. Some vehicles had parked up and people were crossing over the road on foot. He slowed to a crawl and peered over towards the edge of the cliff but couldn't see anything. As he reached a layby on his left, he parked up and went to see what the other people were looking at.

The abyss before him was breath taking. A sheer, three-sided bowl that dropped to jagged rock and the surging sea below. He wasn't sure whether the people had gathered to see the sight of the waves crashing and spumes of white water, or the group of seals bobbing in the troughs just outside the breakers. Either would have been quite a sight, but the drop had been dramatic enough for Grant. He walked back to his car and as he drove away, he glanced at the map on the satnav screen. It simply read: Hell's Mouth. He imagined the entire stretch of coastline had many *Hell's Mouths*, but few would be so close to the road. He crested the hill and as he drove down through the narrow, twisting road and crossed over a bridge, he looked to his right and saw a lighthouse set upon a jagged rock, the waves crashing and surging to the base of the structure, the spume spraying to the top. It wasn't a sight he had ever seen before, and it made him think how static London was. Here, nature moved and changed, and the sights were different every day. He imagined that in a day or two, the lighthouse would be a beacon in a millpond of glassy calm. Next week, a surging storm of grey and woeful inevitability could crash upon the shore, the sky as different as today as it was possible to be. He could smell the freshness here, too. The clean saltiness of the ocean, the dampness of the woods and the pungent smell of seaweed and rotting vegetation of the creeks and rivers could all be experienced within a twenty-minute drive from the north to south coasts of this varied and dramatic county on the southwestern tip of England. After another five miles or so, he joined the A30 at Hayle and headed north. The road was a typical dual carriageway, so nobody stuck to the speed limit until a speed camera sign appeared and more rubber was painted onto the road than white lines. Grant went with the display of local knowledge and slowed down until he had passed the cameras on both sides. He turned off for Camborne soon after.

He parked in an empty bay, looked for the car he had seen DCI Warleggan in earlier, but it wasn't there. That didn't mean he wasn't in the station, most detectives relied heavily on pool cars. He just hoped the man had gone to Bodmin, but he didn't hold out much hope. Warleggan had been positively buoyed by the sight of seeing him in a compromising situation with Mary Hocking. Grant entered the code, but the door did not open. He tried again but was met with the same locked and immobile door. He took out his mobile. The signal was good in Camborne, as in most of the built-up areas. He scrolled down to DS Clark's number and dialled. It was answered on the second ring.

"Where are you?" she asked curtly. "I've been trying to call you all morning."

He frowned, not having seen the missed calls. "I'm outside."

"What, outside the station?"

"Yes."

"You've got to go," she said quickly. "The DCI has been doing some digging on you. He's rather pleased with what he's found, evidently."

Grant's heart skipped a beat. It was inevitable, but he'd hoped he had more time. "Where is he?"

"Out looking for you." There was a muffled pause and when she spoke again it was clearer, but he could tell she was walking quickly. "Get out of here now. Get in your car and wait for my text. I'm texting you the address. I'll meet you there in forty-five minutes."

Grant received her text and typed the postcode and house name into the satnav and drove out through Camborne and back onto the A30. He wasn't on the carriageway for long and came off at North Country, taking the road towards Porthtowan. The road twisted and crested for a few miles, until it widened and dropped steeply down to a village that seemed to have been built in the seventies. There was the occasional typically Cornish stone cottage, but many of the buildings were bungalows and flats. The road threaded past a few shops, then the whole village parted on both sides to reveal the beach and ocean straight ahead. The waves were steaming towards the shore in lines of five or more and breaking across the entire bay. Again, Grant saw surfers heading towards the beach and could see dots behind the breakers. He figured they were surfers this time, not seals.

He looked at the satnav and realised he had to take the left-hand fork in the road. The road was narrow and climbed steeply up the cliff. To his surprise, Lucy Clark's house stood alone and imposing on the cliff. He reversed into one of two spaces and got out of the car. The view was magnificent, but as he turned his back on it and looked at the house, he couldn't help but be impressed. The house was a two-storey stone and glass-fronted property and from the many windows and sheer size, he figured it to have at least three bedrooms. The garden had been turned over to terraced beds and he noted that the grass around the other properties was largely thick with weeds, and he could see the sand through the storks. There was an element of reclaiming wild land, and nature was unrelenting and constant. He imagined storms roaring onshore in the depths of winter, salt spray and sand whipping up the entire valley.

The BMW Z4 sports car threaded up the narrow access road and Grant could see DS Clark clearly behind the wheel. She waved and swung the car next to Grant's Alfa Romeo. The car was a convertible, and the folding metal hardtop unfolded from the boot, reached over her and eased closed, sealing silently shut. She opened the door and got out, walked up to him and smiled. "Let's talk inside," she said.

Grant followed her up the steps. He noted the flush-fitting lights set into each one. The finish to the property was impeccable. He noticed things. It helped in his profession. Sometimes they mattered, sometimes they didn't. He had glanced down the side of the property as he climbed the steps. DS Clark hadn't seen him look that way. Or maybe she had. She was a detective as well. Whether she had or not, he would know once they were inside.

The solid oak door was fitted with two locks and DS Clark opened them both with separate keys. She swung the door open and stepped inside. Grant followed.

"Coffee?" she asked.

"Please."

The flooring was solid and made from hardwood. It echoed off the stone walls. He followed her into the kitchen and watched as she hit a keypad set into the wall next to a coffee machine. He recognised the name as something Italian and similar to the one he had failed to operate successfully back in the Hemingway House. She took two coffee cups out of a rack next to the machine and placed them under two spouts. The machine whizzed and spat, and two dark streams of liquid ran out.

"Cappuccino?" she asked.

"No, an espresso or lungo will be fine," he replied.

She handed him the cup, then tipped her own shot into a larger cup and sprayed in the frothy milk. "Well, you've certainly got the DCI in a flap," she said casually. "He wants to catch up with you. Big time."

"Why," he ventured. He already knew the answer.

"Beats me," she replied.

"Really?" he said, genuinely surprised.

"Yes. He's not sharing. But he wants to find you."

"Officially?"

"Not yet," she said. "He hasn't posted a search or anything."

Grant nodded. He felt a little relived, but not much. "Well, he knows where I'm staying."

"So, what did you find over at Trenvarth Manor?" she asked. "You got into trouble swimming back, by all accounts."

"I told you that I got into trouble. It accounts from nobody else." He sipped some of the thick, strong coffee. He had it down as a Java blend. "So, who told DCI Warleggan?"

"Not me," she replied curtly. "Perhaps your girlfriend did."

"Mary isn't my girlfriend. To be honest, I don't know what she is..."

"I do," she said cuttingly. "She's a whore."

"Ex-whore," he said. "As of an hour ago."

"Really? Well, we'll see about that." She took a mouthful of her cappuccino and left a little frothy milk on her top lip. She licked it off with the tip of her tongue and smiled. "So, what are you... a *fixer* or something? You see a damsel in distress and play the knight in shining armour?"

Grant shrugged. "I am in a position to help. I don't

believe she's dyed in the wool. In fact, I know she's not. I think she will turn her back on that life forever, if she has some help getting out. Why wouldn't I want to help?"

"Well, we all make our beds."

"Speaking of which, you have more than enough beds here," he said. "It's a large house for one."

"I like a lot of room."

"You've got that," he smiled. "Mind if I use your bathroom?"

"No, go ahead. Top of the stairs, third door along."

Grant put down the cup and made his way out into the hall and up the spiral staircase. He knew why she hadn't said left of right. The entire facing wall was tinted glass and looked out on the ocean. He went straight to the first door and saw it was an empty and unmade-up spare room. An open, empty fitted wardrobe and a double bed with a new-looking mattress. The next door opened in on a completely empty room. A fifteen by fifteen with a window looking out on the cliff behind. No curtains or blinds even. He ignored door three and opened the fourth door. The bed was made. The covers were red and there were scented candles all around and a box of matches within handy reach. A digital wireless speaker for smartphones or iPods. There was a flat-screen TV with a built-in DVD player mounted on the wall and a selection of DVDs on the dresser. He didn't have to look too closely at the covers to see they were hard-core pornography. On the bedside table were wet-wipes, tissues and an onyx bowl filled with a variety of condoms. Grant opened the drawer, closed it quickly. A selection of sex toys, but he knew he would find those already. He stepped out and closed the door behind him. He opened door three, the bathroom, and pushed the flush and ran the tap. It was important to keep up pretences. He walked back down the stairs and out into the lounge. He looked at the view and seriously doubted anyone could ever become bored of it. He could hear her behind him. "How long have you lived here..." He didn't finish the sentence, just felt the dull thud on the back of his neck and a stab of pain run down his spine. He was aware that he was falling forwards and unable to break his fall but was unconscious before he hit the solid wooden floor.

Chapter Twenty-Three

His eyes had become accustomed to the gloom. At first it had been as black as pitch. And then there had been bursts of orange and red. He knew he had been moving, and he knew from the smell of fumes and the sound of the engine and exhausts that he was in the boot of a car. His head had knocked against the bulkhead, and each time the vehicle braked, he was pressed into the back of the rear seats. The glow had come from the brake lights, and uncomfortable though the experience of braking was, he welcomed the ambient glow over the oppression of the dark.

Grant kicked and fought at first. His hands were bound tightly behind his back, and he could feel the tape digging into his flesh and the adhesive tugging at the hairs on the back of his wrists. His struggle dislodged part of the trim inside the boot, exposing the rear light cluster. It didn't let in much light but what little it did was constant and brought a welcome respite. There was no telling how long he had been unconscious, but he would have guessed that from first waking in the darkness of the boot of the car to the vehicle parking up on what felt like rough ground, was no more than twenty minutes. He had heard the door slam and then another car door opening and closing. The other car had sped away, some loose gravel hitting the car he was inside. He tried to remain calm, but his nerves were getting away from him. Was that it? Was he parked somewhere so remote that his fate was already sealed? That he would die from asphyxia, thirst or starvation? Which one of the three would kill him first? His subconscious played the odds, although he tried to put the thoughts out of his mind altogether. He thought of his daughter, but to his despair he could not picture her face. He vowed there and then to go the extra mile to see her, damn his ex-wife, damn the solicitor and his letters and court orders. If only he could get out and get free. He would run and never look back. All the way to Chloe's front door. He thrust his feet out in rage and kicked more of the trim away. There was no extra light to be gleaned from it, but it relieved his frustration somewhat.

Time was superfluous. Minutes, hours. He had no idea. He was cramping up in his legs, his hamstrings taught and unyielding. He supposed hours had passed when he heard a car approaching. The car manoeuvred on the gravel and the engine died. Grant could hear a second vehicle. There were doors opening and closing. Muffled voices, indeterminable from the confines of the boot. One of the vehicles drove away again. Grant screamed for help. He was desperate and kicked out at the bulkhead, then changed to thrusting his knees against the boot lid. He changed methods again, getting greater purchase by bracing his left knee against the bulkhead and thrusting out with his right. He continued his cries for help, every breath, every ounce of energy being put into making himself heard.

There was a sharp bang on the boot lid. Then two more.

A man's voice, deep, but no regional accent. "Shut up!" he shouted. "Nobody can hear you up here!" Three more bangs on the lid.

Grant's heart sunk. He had already stopped banging and shouting, his heart was pounding as he fought for breath. The air was stale and felt thick and hot. He knew he was using up oxygen faster than it could get into the confines of the boot.

"I'm opening the boot," the voice said. "I have an axe. Try anything and I will stove your bloody head in." The tone was confident. A man who was used to giving orders and getting his own way.

The boot-lid clicked open and the shaft of light which poured through blinded him. He squinted, struggled to see anything at all as the lid opened further and the man stepped back cautiously. Grant blinked and looked up at the man, having never felt so vulnerable in his life. He was scared but he knew that he needed to overcome the fear and look at every angle and opportunity available to him. He needed to find a way, somehow, to avoid the inevitable. He could see Chloe's face clearly now, as if his daughter had projected herself into his mind and had given him an extra reason to live. And she had. He wouldn't give up, not without a fight.

"Who are you?" he asked. He had to start somewhere.

"The last person you're going to see." The man stepped further back, his hands clutching the axe so tightly his knuckles had turned white.

"Did you say that to the Hafeez family?"

"I said get out."

"To them?"

"To you, dickhead!"

"So, what about them?" Grant asked. He still hadn't moved.

"I said a lot."

Grant looked at him, took in every detail he could. He had honed this skill in counterterrorism. Every detail should be logged; all information was useful. The man was six-two and slim. Grant guessed around eleven stone. He would have a stone and a half or perhaps two stone on him, and that counted if it came down to a struggle. But it didn't count for much with his hands bound behind his back.

The man was also smartly dressed. Grant didn't own suits as smart as this. Not on his salary. There was a plain watch with a leather strap on the man's left wrist. The watch was extremely thin. So delicate that it looked at odds with the axe. He couldn't see from this distance, but he guessed at a Patek Philippe. Grant had never seen prices on them in jewellers' windows, which had always told him they were out of his reach.

"But you killed them," Grant said flatly.

The man nodded. "Now get out."

"Why did you kill them?"

The man shrugged. "Business."

"Feel good did it, to take a person's life?"

"You tell me." He smiled. "You know what it's like. You may say you don't, but we all know. You fooled no one!"

Grant hesitated. The comment had side-swiped him. He regained composure as best he could. "You killed a *family*. You killed a mother, a father and four young women. Girls, really..."

"You killed *somebody's* child. We're all somebody's children..." the man smiled. "But it wasn't just me."

"Who else?"

The man smirked. "No, no, no," he said quietly. "Get out of the car and kneel down."

"Make me," Grant said defiantly.

The man shrugged like it was no big deal and swung the axe. He used the back edge, and it came crashing down on Grant's lower right leg. He screamed an agonising wail, stabs of white-hot pain shooting up his leg. He clenched his teeth, realised he had stopped breathing. The pain was excruciating and seemed all the worse for the simple fact he could not reach out and touch it, exacerbated by the tape around his wrists.

"How's that for starters?" the man sneered. He spun the axe in his hands, the blade spinning and catching the light. "Now get out, or I'll start chopping you up where you lay..."

Grant kicked his legs until he got them over the edge of the boot space and dangling over the rear bumper. He struggled to sit up and the man watched him battle the angle, the boot-lid and the rise of the opening itself. He seemed bored and reached in and pulled him by his collar. He stepped back when Grant was upright. He was breathless, his leg feeling as if it were on fire, yet at the same time, numb and lifeless. He could see a car parked broadside to them. It was a new model Porsche 911 in gleaming gun-metal grey. It went well with the suit and the watch.

"Stand up and walk to the driver's door," the man said. Grant turned around, finding it difficult to put weight on his leg. He realised that the car that had been his prison was his own. That made it seem all the worse somehow. But his thoughts were cast aside when he saw the view in front of him. The front wheels of the Alfa Romeo were just a few feet from the edge of a cliff every bit as sheer and dramatic looking as Hell's Mouth. He could see the rollers breaking and hear the crash of the waves on the rocks below. "The surfers call this place Chough's Haven. They climb down with ropes, or paddle around the point to surf here. But the conditions must be right. No good today. The wind and tide are all wrong," the man said. "So, nobody will disturb us up here..."

Grant had been twisting his wrists. Working at the strong tape. He was past hoping he could break free. Perhaps he could damage his skin to leave enough evidence to show that his end had been foul play. Again, Chloe's face came to him. The once cloudy memory of her giving him hope and the fact that he had more to fight for, more to live for than the meagre existence he had been living since losing everything he held dear through drink and poor decisions. The thoughts of his daughter and his desire to make things up to her seemed to be willing a fight from him.

The man opened the driver's door as wide as it would go and stood back. "Get into the car," he said coldly.

"It won't look like an accident," Grant said.

"Let me worry about that. There's no beach here. Even at low tide there's six feet of water at the base of the cliff. The surf comes from the reef further out. Maybe your car will never be found. Winter is coming and the surfing won't be great here. Too dangerous for much of the time. Maybe the crabs will have stripped you to the bone by next spring..."

"But perhaps not. Look, my wrists are bound," Grant paused. "I'm telling you; it won't look like an accident. Have you even thought this through?"

"Of course!"

"You're not the brains of the outfit, are you..." he stated sardonically. "You're the monkey. Where's the organ grinder?"

"You shut your face!"

"No gloves," said Grant. "When you first drove me here, you didn't have gloves, did you," he laughed. "So, there are second-person prints in and on the car. DNA also. I have an injury not conducive to the crash or fall. They will see the blunt end of that axe head imprinted on my skin and deep bruising in the muscle. It won't match anything in the cabin of the car. Seriously, who has set you up for this? Who's the organ grinder to your dumb monkey?"

The man caught hold of Grant and pushed his face close to his. "I said, shut your face..."

The man didn't get to finish his sentence because Grant snapped his head forwards and head-butted him on his nose. The crunch was sickening. The man recoiled backwards but caught himself on the open door and didn't fall and nor could he move away. Grant followed with another snap of his head, his forehead hitting the ruined nose again and smashing it flat. Blood and mucous left the wound in a sickly-looking clot and the man fell onto his knees. Grant checked his balance, steadied himself against the car, then thrust his knee up and under the man's chin. His head whipped up and he fell back against the door again.

Whether it was rage, or whether it was his sense of survival – threatened by his hands still being bound – but Grant did not stop kicking. Nor stamping. By the time he regained control, the man was limp and motionless. His eyes were open, and his head lolled at an unnatural angle. There was no doubt about it, the man was dead. Grant was heaving for breath and perspiring heavily from his brow. He leaned back against the car, his legs felt like jelly and his right leg throbbed from the pain of the axe head striking him. Adrenalin was catching up with him and it was all he could do to remain upright. He took several deep breaths, so deep that his lungs could not take any more. He exhaled slowly and steadily through his mouth, then inhaled again through his nose. It had a calming, steadying effect. He did this methodically for half a dozen breaths. His heartrate lowered and the feeling of light-headedness from the rush of adrenalin subsided.

"I'm coming for you, Chloe..." he said quietly. He looked around for the axe. It was behind the car door and just a foot from the cliff edge. The full horror of his fate lay in front of him. A vertical drop of at least three-hundred feet to the surging sea below, with jagged rocks the size of family cars breaking the water's surface. He felt the effects of vertigo as he stood on one leg and eased the axe back from the edge with his right foot. The pain was almost intolerable. When he was a safe distance from the precipice, he used his heel to drag the axe back through the seagrass and sandy earth.

Positioning the axe proved difficult, verging on the impossible and he almost abandoned the idea several times. Part of him wanted to simply walk away and find help, but another part, albeit a small but significant part of him, a part his councillor had referred to as the 'darkness' wanted more. Grant knew it was there, had battled it all his life. He knew he was a fundamentally good person and wanted to help people who were unable to help themselves. But he also knew, and had become comfortable with the fact, that he could get to his ultimate goal by any means possible.

He had pressed the back edge of the axe into the ground using one foot to guide the shaft of the axe and another to sink it into the soft, sandy earth. He had then squatted carefully, painfully over the horizontal shaft and dropped down into a sitting position. It had taken three attempts, each time he had doggedly clambered back up and pressed the axe further into the soil. On his fourth attempt the axe remained firmly pressed into the earth. He shuffled backwards, got his hands in place, and started to rub the tape on the blade. As he suspected, the axe was about as sharp as a spoon. The sheer weight of the head, length of the shaft and tapering vee of the blade was what got the job done against stubborn logs. He did not have to fear cutting himself on the blade, but after what seemed like an age, friction finally got the better of the tape and combined with the pressure of his attempt to splay his arms, the bonds finally tore apart.

Chapter Twenty-Four

Sat at the very edge of the cliff, he watched the sea surge and froth at the bottom of Hell's Mouth. He could see the seals and seabirds bobbing on the swells behind the breakers. There was a lot of seaweed draping off the smooth, wet rocks below and the fronds of weed swayed hypnotically with the ebb and flow of the tide. He figured the seals enjoyed protection from people disturbing their habitat, thwarted by the inaccessibility of the steep three-sided cliffs.

There were no walkers, no sightseers parking up to look down into the abyss. There was a single parked car in front of his own, and so far, he had seen no one. He decided to take the chance and stood up. He stretched casually, taking in the area in every direction. Satisfied he was alone for now, he bent down and caught hold of the handle of the axe. Another glance around, and he heaved the axe out into the air in front of him. He watched as it spun end over end and travelled a shallow arc before dropping straight down to the sea. Grant saw an indistinct splash between two breakers and nothing more.

He watched for a moment longer and found himself staring at the sea, his thoughts concentrating on nothing more than the events on the cliff top less than five miles away. The man had asked him what it felt like to kill someone. And now he knew. But he had known before, and he had known what it was to live with such things.

You know what it's like. You may say you don't, but we all know. You fooled no one...

Chapter Twenty-Five

Eight weeks earlier
Westminster Bridge, London

The slash on his shoulder stung like a hundred wasp stings. He could feel the blood running down his back, or maybe it was sweat. Jafri's breath was foul, along with his body odour. Grant gripped the man's wrist like it was a lifeline, which indeed it was. He had the knife in his control. If he let it go, then Jafri would be more dangerous. And in practical terms, the blade was plugging the wound until the SCO19 boys got here, and the paramedics would have been called already for the injured civilians, they wouldn't be too far behind.

Jafri was grunting with the effort of resisting Grant forcing him backwards, he had still been chanting his prayer, but Grant had become oblivious to the noise, concentrating only on the knife and keeping him from getting control of it in the fight. Jafri cannoned into the railings and stopped. The knife travelled deeper into Grant's stomach, and he rode right up against the man. He grimaced, and Jafri grinned fleetingly, but Grant snapped his head forwards and smashed his forehead into the man's nose. He wrapped his right arm around him, caught hold of the back of his head and head-butted twice more, pulling the man's head forwards to increase the force. Jafri's eyes watered, and his nose bled as it shattered spreading across his face. Grant knew the pain the man would have felt, and keeping his grip on the man's wrist, his fingers digging into the tendons, his nails ripping the flesh, he brought his knee up into the man's groin. Jafri let out a gasp of air, wet with mucous and blood, and Grant could hear the shouted commands of the first of the armed police officers as they arrived on the scene. Jafri pushed Grant, his grip still on the handle of the dagger, and Grant shoved back harder. He felt Jafri's foot connect with his groin, and the man gripped him behind his head also. They toppled, the wind tugging at their clothing as they fell.

Grant had felt the sensation before, many times, diving from ten-metre boards as a teen. Internal organs rising with the fall, a displacement that seemed to last longer than was imaginable for the distance involved. Jafri screamed, and Grant guessed it was the man's first time. The knife had come clear, and Grant had released his grip on the man as they fell. Grant tucked and turned it into a dive worthy of just one point. It was better than the Pakistani's though, who hit the water flat on his back. The water was cold, icily so, despite being early-summer, and as Grant made for the surface, he could see only a few feet before the gloom became total darkness.

Jafri had landed flat and gone shallower. He was clawing at the surface when Grant came up. He was flailing wildly. The current was strong, Grant could feel the drift and noticed the Houses of Parliament passing rapidly by them. He glanced upwards. The Westminster Bridge was no longer above them, already fifty-metres distant.

"Help me!" Jafri blurted, wildly flailing his limbs. His voice was wet, thick with panic and a mouthful of filthy water. "I can't swim!" he screamed, his voice cut off as he dropped below the surface, then re-emerged, mid-sentence, "...elp me!"

Grant took a few strokes towards him. His stomach contorted in agony, like cramp in tired, over-worked muscles, sharp jolts of pain tearing at his senses. The water was high in salt content because of the incoming tide, and dark and pungent smelling with pollution. The stab wound had been both broad and deep. He could feel warmth on his skin, the blood swirling around his flesh, numbed and cold from the icy brown water of the Thames.

Grant circled around Jafri, so the man couldn't pull at him in a panic. He wrapped his right arm around him and started to kick for the South Bank. He felt the man relax after a few strokes.

"Kick, you bastard!" Grant shouted. "You're not getting a fucking free ride..."

Jafri laughed, water hit his face and he coughed and gagged. "This is why you will lose. You are weak. Therefore, you people will always lose," he spat contemptuously. He coughed again. Grant could tell he was spitting out some water. "I did what I did, and again, you were not ready! Unarmed police... eunuchs protecting the masses... dickless and ineffective." Jafri spluttered, but he had started to kick, adding some momentum to their progress. "I saw you in court. Your evidence was what got me off, you hid details and it made you look like a liar. I thank you for that, without you, I would not have won this great victory for Allah. I did what I did, killed those people, children... and *still* you save me from drowning! There is no victory for you, no way you will win your war on Islam. Our jihad will be total..."

Grant stopped stroking with his left hand, swivelled his feet to tread water. He looked at the bridge, now one-hundred metres distant. There were officers on the bank some seventy metres distant. Someone had a life-ring and was uncoiling a length of rope. Grant thought about the woman and the child he had seen, heads all but severed. The blood. So much blood, it seemed unimaginable. He glanced back at the riverbank. The man had got the rope uncoiled and was taking a throw. It fell way short, so he was frantically pulling it back in for another attempt.

Grant spun Jafri around. The man tried to grab onto him, but he smashed his fist into the Jafri's sternum and the man wheezed and went limp in his arms. Grant ducked down and pulled Jafri with him by his belt. He kept one hand on the belt and gripped the other around the man's neck. He powered downwards, kicking his feet and releasing some breath to counter his buoyancy and control his descent. Jafri flailed his limbs and stared at him, panic upon his face, and from the speed and ease at which they descended, Grant could tell that the man had not taken a breath before going under. Grant swam downwards, his face just two feet from Jafri's the entire time. It was darker, just ten feet below the surface, but he could still see the panic in the man's eyes just in front of him.

Despite the pain in his stomach and his shoulder, Grant remained calm. In university, on the water polo team, he could hold his breath for a full four minutes. He imagined he could still manage half of that, all these years later. He swam twice a week, forty lengths or so each session. He always did a few single twenty-five metre lengths underwater. He released a little more air, levelling out his ballast. Jafri had gone from panic to realisation, to acceptance. When he took in a deep, liquid breath, his eyes bulged, and he gasped like a fish on the riverbank. Grant pulled him close to look him in the eyes. The water had blurred his vision, but he could see the life leaving them. When Jafri went completely still, Grant spun him over, then pushed him downwards towards the bottom of the Thames and the secrets it held. He brought his feet down on Jafri's back and used the corpse as a springboard to push himself towards the surface.

Chapter Twenty-Six

Sixty-days...

"By Christ let me make it to sixty-one..." Grant muttered quietly.

He wasn't a religious man, but he did ask the Lord for occasional help. He had taken all the steps on his path to recovering, but the Alcoholics Anonymous sobriety program relied heavily upon spiritual guidance, something he had struggled with at first, but later became more relaxed with. He used his daughter as his focus and asked a higher entity for help from time to time, even if he did not actually intend to swing from agnostic through to believer. He wasn't arrogant enough to be an atheist, just practical enough to require further proof. In times of despair, asking for a little extra help certainly couldn't hurt. In good times he gave no further thought to the matter.

He watched DCI Warleggan leave the building. The man looked shabby. Overweight and untidy, a lethargic gait. He was a worried man or should be. His career of late had more than enough discrepancies. He doubted the detective had always been this way, decisions were everything and there had to have been a watershed moment. A point where a line was crossed, and the descent was made. Grant had read the man's file. He knew that moment, or at least he could cross-reference with the other files he had taken from the man's computer when DS Clark had been the last to leave the office. Or second to last.

Grant got out of the car and stood calmly beside it. He closed the door sharply and DCI Warleggan looked up. Casually at first, but then he seemed to compute. He looked at the car, then at Grant and his face fell. He seemed to grow taller, broaden and when he walked over, it was with a renewed vigour.

"You faked it!" he shouted. As he walked closer, he lowered his voice accordingly, but he glared nothing but anger and hatred. "Or that old bastard Maitland did..."

"You won't talk about him like that," Grant said quietly.

"The old sod's dead," Warleggan paused. "You never said he was dead either."

"You never asked."

"You thought I'd see through it if I knew he was dead," he said. "Thought I'd deduce something was amiss."

"Having seen your work, I never thought you'd deduce a damned thing..."

Warleggan scoffed. "So, who faked it?" he asked. "You or him?"

Grant thought for a moment. It couldn't hurt and the trail would be as cold as Maitland's body. "He did, I guess."

"So, you're not *Acting* Superintendent then?"

"No. Just a lowly DCI," Grant said. "Like yourself."

The man looked at him coldly. "And you're not even down here officially? You don't have the authorisation?"

"No."

"I know. I checked. You're still on sick leave."

Warleggan looked like he didn't know whether to laugh or cry. Grant figured a little of both. "No wonder you didn't want the letter photocopied. So, what, you ran it off on a computer, copied and pasted the headed paper and forged the signatures?"

"You don't hear so well," Grant smiled. "Commander Maitland provided me with the papers," he lied. "I thought they were originals."

"I bet." He looked at him, seeming to decide his next action. "I could arrest you," he said.

Grant shrugged. "You could. But I'd only be out as soon as my brief looked at the letter. It's a highly convincing forgery. And I seem to remember thinking it wasn't legitimate earlier today, since then, I've been driving around thinking what to do. A real dilemma. I've been taking in the sights, thinking it all through. Then thought I would come and see you personally," he said. "Which is why I'm here at Camborne police station, hoping to speak to you before the end of your shift." He looked at his watch. "I take it you want to leave on time?"

"Well, fuck off then," Warleggan said. "Fuck off back up country and don't come back." He turned and walked across the carpark to his vehicle.

"Warleggan!" Grant called after him. "What about the exhumation? Just tell me what you found..."

DCI Warleggan turned around and looked at him for a moment. He shrugged and said, "They weren't there. You were right all along. Somebody took their bodies..."

Chapter Twenty-Seven

Grant pulled the car up onto the drive at the Hemingway House. There were two cars parked in front of him. One was Mary's Mini Cooper and the other was a sign-written Ford Focus from a domiciliary care agency. The lights were on inside and he could see a woman in a nurse's uniform talking to Mary through the kitchen window. He opened the door and smiled at the two women, then looked at Mary.

"Sorted?"

She beamed a smile. "There's a place for her at Pol-an-Garrick. It's lovely and Marie here has helped me with the paperwork for funding and means-testing."

The woman nodded. "And there will be an initial payment, you say?"

"Yes," Grant said. "To cover matters until the funding is in place. It will be transferred tomorrow. Three months, top tier caring. We'll advise the office tomorrow; all we need are the home's bank account and sort code."

"I have that here," she said, placing a card on the table.

Mary was so happy; she was positively glowing. She

sidled up to Grant, rested her head on his shoulder, wrapped an arm around his waist. "Thank you," she said.

Grant nodded, seeming a little uncomfortable with the gesture.

"Well, if there's nothing else?"

"No, that's it," Mary said. "I'll give you a hand."

The two women walked into the lounge and the old lady looked up at them. She had a cup of tea and a biscuit and was looking extremely confused.

"Mum, we're getting you into the car now," Mary said slowly. It was evident her mother was hard of hearing. "Marie is going to take you to your new home at Pol-an-Garrick."

"But I liked it at The Richmond," she said. "All my friends are there. Is this your house, Mary?"

"No, Mum," she said patiently. She had explained it before. "This is a friend's house. Meet Grant, Mum."

"Are you and Mary courting?" the old lady said, a twinkle escaping her eye.

Grant shook his head as both Mary and Marie lifted the old woman under her arms and eased her up. "No," he said. "We're just friends."

"That's what we all used to say," she replied. She tapped her nose when she was upright. "I know how it is," she winked. She had Mary's eyes. They were glossy and full of vigour, despite the frailty of her body.

Grant smiled and nodded a goodbye as the two women helped her along and out into the kitchen. He walked over to the window and watched the jetty on the other side of the creek. The sun was low in the sky and the creek was choppy, a cold wind blowing in from the sea. He watched the buoys bobbing, noticed that further down river there were less boats than when he had first arrived. Each day there had been less and less. He supposed that there were no boats moored this far upriver in the winter.

Mary walked in, a glass of wine in her left hand, a coffee for Grant in her right. "Here," she said, handing the coffee to him. "Are you alright if I have this?"

"Of course," he said. "Why wouldn't I be?" he added defensively.

"I noticed, that's all."

"Oh," he replied quietly. "Well, we all have our secrets."

"Isn't that the truth..." she said flatly.

"So, are you ready?"

"Ten minutes to fix myself up and I will be."

"No, I didn't mean that," he said. "I meant, are you *ready*?"

"Oh, I am," she said decisively. "It's time."

Chapter Twenty-Eight

Grant showed his ticket through the open window of the Alfa Romeo and nodded at the security guard as he pointed towards a row of cars nearer the great house. He stared up at the house as he neared. It had started to rain. A misty drizzle that the Cornish called *mizzle*. It was greasy on the windscreen, and he worked the wipers which seemed to make it worse. The house was lit up with spotlights pointing directly at it. Ostentatious to say the least, but perhaps they had been rigged for the event. The house was a Georgian manor, painted white with twenty windows running along both the first, second floors and third floors and a series of large bay windows and solid oak doors on the ground floor, the centre of which was taken up by the imposing granite steps to the front entrance.

"Did you come here often," Grant paused, looking at Mary seated beside him. She was wearing a tastefully cut red dress which showed off her figure. It brought out the red of her hair. "You know, when..."

"Sometimes," she said. "His wife rides horses. Dressage and showing. She's quite often away with her groom at shows all over the country. Roebuck wasn't bothered about me staying over. He didn't seem to care what the staff saw."

"Until his wife found out."

Mary sighed. "That changed everything. Don't get me wrong, I felt for her, but he soon showed his true colours. What he did, I wouldn't wish on a single soul."

He didn't answer. He knew how people could be. He'd spent his life hunting those who would do harm others. Grant parked up and switched off the engine. "Ready?" he asked.

"It's time," she smiled. "Thank you. I wouldn't have been strong enough for this, without you."

The gravel was thick and crunched underfoot. As they reached the highly polished granite steps, Mary looked nervously at Grant and reached out for his hand. He took it and gave a little squeeze. At the top of the steps, he saw Keith Davey shaking hands with arrivals and engaging in small talk. Grant noticed him handing out his business cards. Obviously not one to let charity get in the way of business. After all, everyone here probably owned a property. Mary's grip tightened. Grant squeezed back, then released. He took the invitation out of his suit jacket. He noticed the other men were wearing tuxedos. He couldn't have cared less. He'd have his tie rolled up and in his pocket before the first plate of canapés came out from the kitchen.

He showed his invitation to a middle-aged woman in a ball gown. He'd printed his tickets off but noticed most of the guests were just showing their smartphones. He hadn't trusted the Cornish mobile phone signal. The woman admitting the guests wore a name tag: Felicity Roebuck. She was what he would have described as 'horsey'. She would have been late-fifties and had lived an outdoor life interspersed with drinking a great deal of champagne and wine at parties and events like this one. It would not have been a stretch to see why Claude Roebuck had had his head turned by Mary. They stepped closer and he noticed she did not bat an eyelid when she looked at Mary. Perhaps they had never met. Mary hesitated, looked worried at the prospect of being this close to the woman whose husband she had slept with for over a year. Felicity Roebuck took their tickets and smiled at them both. "Enjoy your evening," she said with a smile and then looked past them both at the couple behind them.

"I take it you never met the wife," Grant said quietly.

"No."

Grant caught Keith Davey's eye and walked over. The man had a faint recognition of him, and Grant could see he was trying to place his face. "This morning," Grant said. "The property in Portreath..." He turned to Mary. "It *is* Portreath, isn't it?"

She stepped out around him and smiled. "Yes, that's right."

Davey looked at Mary, and it was easy to see he was lost for words. His hawk-like eyes looked her up and down with distaste.

Grant held out his hand and Davey shook it. Grant didn't release, gripped tighter. "Freemason?"

Davey hesitated. "No..."

"No? I would swear that's a freemason's handshake," Grant paused, squeezing a little harder. "The way you've linked your finger. Like if I hooked my middle finger, we'd have had a little handshake within a handshake thing going on..."

Davey shook his head. His weasel-like features did not hide the fact he was scared and unsure what was going on.

"No, I..." he stopped and winced. "You're actually hurting me now."

Grant ignored him and smiled through gritted teeth. "So, what would I get out of being a freemason? I've always been intrigued."

"I said you're hurting me!" Davey shouted.

Grant squeezed some more. He watched the man's legs buckle and he dropped around six inches in height. "A secret club. A mafia for the underachiever and the over-looked. The mediocrity of the working and lower-middle classes, bolstered by the belief they have made it to a social elite. Am I right?" Grant smiled and shook his head. "No, I couldn't join," he said. "I certainly wouldn't want to join any club who would have me as a member," he laughed. He had enough strength to double the pressure he had on Davey's hand. He knew the man's curled-up finger would be squashing in on itself. "You've met my date, by all accounts."

Davey sneered. "Who hasn't?" he managed to goad.

"It's over," Grant said.

"We'll see about that."

Grant kept up the pressure, pulled Davey's hand towards him. "Her mother is no longer in the home. She's away from both yours and Roebuck's influence..."

"Did I hear my name?" Roebuck dropped down a set of thickly carpeted stairs and stopped in his tracks when he saw Mary. "What the bloody hell..."

Grant eyed Roebuck as he gripped with all his might and Davey's middle finger snapped with an audible 'crack'. He released his hand as the man dropped to his knees and howled. People were staring, but they hadn't stopped drinking the free champagne. Grant extended his hand to Roebuck.

"I didn't recognise you without my telescopic sight," Roebuck said dryly. He stared hard at Grant and accepted his hand. There was no secret finger and Grant kept the pressure to about normal. Well, perhaps a little firmer.

"I didn't think you recognised what was in your sights?" Grant said. "Or perhaps you did and you're just a lousy shot."

Roebuck scoffed, looked at Mary. "Hello, my dear. Trading down?"

She shook her head. "No, just keeping better company."

Grant looked at Davey. The man was cradling his disjointed and broken finger and doing his best to stand. He was perspiring and his face had turned red. "You'll find some ice for that at the bar, I'd imagine..."

"So, what is all this about?" Roebuck asked incredulously. "You show up at a private gathering with my ex-lover on your arm and my wife at the door." He paused, looking at Mary and smiled thinly. "I take it making me feel ill at ease is part of some elaborate and spiteful revenge for being unceremoniously dumped, my dear?" He watched as Keith Davey walked away. He clicked his fingers at a waiter and the man walked over with a tray of champagne-filled flutes. Roebuck took one and handed it to Mary. She accepted it and took a sip. He took two more and handed one to Grant. He watched as Grant accepted it, but held it away from him, looking for somewhere to put it down. "Bottoms up," Roebuck said, eying him closely. He smiled and looked at the waiter. "Kindly take that off my guest and go and fetch him an orange juice," he said curtly. "He obviously doesn't seem to appreciate the finer things in life..." He manged to end his sentence looking at Mary.

Grant put the glass back on the tray. He could feel the heat rising in his neck. He looked towards the staircase, noticed Pete Bunt walking down in an ill-fitting and cheap looking grey suit. Bunt sneered back at him and waited at the foot of the stairs.

"You don't *own* people," Grant said, looking back at Roebuck. "You had your fun. You had an affair and you got caught."

Roebuck shrugged. "What was the price of convenience?" he asked, looking at Mary. "What did you get from our little dalliance?"

"You covered my mother's bills in The Richmond," she replied. "It wasn't the price of our affair. It was because of what I found one day. I went to visit my mother in the council run nursing home, and she had messed herself and was sat in her own faeces and still in front of the previous night's empty dishes at eleven in the morning. She had been calling for attention for hours! I told you all of this, explained that her finances were in a poor state, and you offered her a room in one of *your* nursing homes..."

"My finest home," he interrupted.

"This was months after we started seeing each other! Some girls ask for jewellery and clothes and expensive gifts when they have affairs with married men. I never asked you for a thing! I shared this with you because I was so upset, and you jumped straight in and offered to give her a place at The Richmond. After what I'd seen of the state-funded home, what was I going to do?"

Roebuck laughed. "It's not my problem!"

"She never said it was," Grant said coldly. "What *is* your problem is the enforced slavery you have kept her in ever since your split. An unwilling participant to the sex trade."

"What!" he exclaimed, then looked at them both

conspiratorially as people started to look over. "I've never heard such rot!"

Bunt walked over. "Trouble, boss?"

"None that I can't handle," Roebuck replied dismissively.

"I'll wait around," he said. "Just in case..."

"We're really scared!" Mary said, but she'd managed to make it sound like something a teen would shout in the playground.

"You should be..." Bunt smirked. "I'll bloody-well make sure of it." Grant took a step forward, but Bunt smiled and closed the gap. "Anytime, mate..."

Grant stared the man in his eyes, in the light of the great hall, he could see the man's affliction to his eye. The condition was called coloboma and the misshapen iris was clearly visible. There was no doubt this was the man who had held him at gunpoint, beaten him in Hemingway House. "It will be different if I'm not tied up and you're not pointing a shotgun at me," Grant growled.

"Don't bet on it," Bunt sneered back. "We'll just have to wait and see."

"Thank you, Pete," Roebuck said hastily. "I'll call you if I need you."

"You'll do no such thing," Grant snapped. "I'm a police officer making inquiries into an investigation..."

"Who has wantonly broken my business associate's finger in front of me," Roebuck chided. "You could lose your job for that kind of assault."

"I've done worse..."

"Oh, we all know that DCI Grant. I've seen the news footage. You did a pretty terrible job of saving that suspected terrorist fellow." Roebuck held up his hands and smiled. "Don't get me wrong, you should still have got the medal for drowning him…"

Grant was rattled. He had been cleared of all wrongdoing, but what he had insisted was his failure to rescue the man was seen by many for what it was. He could never admit to what he had done, and the tabloid press hadn't helped him douse the flames, calling him a public hero and printing close-up photographs of his apparent struggle at the end. "Jafri wasn't a *suspected* terrorist. He killed people, maimed others and stabbed me…" Grant stared at Roebuck, whose expression had changed suddenly. Grant turned around and saw why. Felicity Roebuck was walking towards them, a frown upon her face. He looked at Mary then back at Claude Roebuck. "This should be interesting."

Roebuck looked at them both. "Whatever this is about, I'll talk it through in my study," he paused, glancing at his watch. "Say, in half an hour?"

"Works for me," Grant said. He held out an elbow and Mary wrapped her arm into it. "Let's get a drink," he said, then smiled. "Scrap that, let's just find some better company…"

They found Davey at the self-service bar. Most of the people were still on the champagne in the great hall and hadn't made it this far into the house. A man was leaving with two orange juices and nodded at them both as they walked in. Davey had his finger in a glass of ice and three-finger's worth of single malt in his other hand. He sipped it and stared at them as they approached.

"Mary won't be doing that kind of work again," Grant said. He picked up a can of Diet Coke, pulled the tab and poured it into a glass. He took a glass of white wine off a tray and handed it to Mary. "So how does it work?" he asked, then ventured.

"Roebuck buys out the old and infirm from their homes for next to no money and a place in one of his residential homes. You get the houses developed or decorated and refurbished and rented out or sold. But either way, you have a list of vacant properties to run as pop-up brothels. You know which properties will be empty and where will be most convenient for the clients. Unhurried sex in luxurious, safe surroundings."

Davey sneered. "It's not *technically* illegal. If only one woman works there, the sex is consensual and only one punter, or client, attends, then it's not classified as a brothel. He can give money to whom he likes as a gift..."

Grant balled his fist, Davey noticed and stepped backwards. Grant had him pinned between the self-service bar and the corner of the room. "So, help me, I'll knock your bloody block off... It's not consensual when blackmail is being involved!"

"Hey, I just provide the properties!" He looked at Mary. "That's all I do. I get a call, I'm given some locations and I come up with the property. I meet the girl and give her the keys. I don't arrange anything else."

"What's your cut?"

He shrugged. "Twenty-five percent of the take."

"Which adds up to what?"

"I think I need to talk to my lawyer." He took out his mobile phone and dialled. "If I'm being questioned officially..." A ringtone was clearly audible and both Keith Davey and Mary looked at Grant. He looked back at Davey and slowly took the ringing phone out of his jacket pocket. He looked at the screen. It identified Keith Davey on the caller ID. Davey hung up. He frowned and asked, "What the hell are you doing with John's phone?"

"We met earlier," Grant said casually. "So, he's your brief?"

Davey nodded. "I don't understand why you have his phone though," he said.

Grant shrugged. "We met earlier. I'll be getting it back to him later," he said. He thumbed the screen and scrolled down, pressed the call button. Mary's phone rang in her purse. He looked at her as she reached for her phone, she hesitated. "Go on, I want to see the caller's ID," he said. She took out the phone and showed it to him. It simply read: Bastard. "Well, well. I take it this is your fixer. Or pimp, would be a better description."

"It is," she said coldly.

Grant thought about the man in the suit with the hundred-thousand-pound Porsche and the watch which probably cost even more. He thought about the axe in the man's hands and what he was going to do to him. Then he thought of the man's face, battered and bloodied. His body lying deathly still. "So, your, *pimp*," he said to Mary, then looked at Davey, "And your solicitor are the same guy?" Davey looked worried. Mary just looked confused. "I don't think the Law Society would like the idea of a lawyer forcing a woman to have sex in return for simply keeping her mother in a care home. No, I think that would be frowned on very much indeed."

"He's a lawyer?" Mary asked.

"Looks that way."

"But he worked for Roebuck. He's the one who said my mother could continue to stay at The Richmond, but only if I did *that* for them..."

"And that was your price?" Davey looked at her incredulously.

"No," she said. "He said that my mother may well come to harm if I didn't. That a pillow could be put over her face in the middle of the night, or an accidental overdose of painkillers might be administered if I didn't keep doing it..."

Davey smirked. "And the money didn't hurt either," he scoffed.

"I never saw a penny," she said curtly.

Davey sneered. "Well, if you ever fancy a quick fifty-quid..."

He never finished the sentence. Grant punched him straight in the nose with a right jab, followed it up with a left hook and a right cross. Davey was out cold and fell behind the bar, wedged against the wall. There was a table nearby, Grant supposed for empty glasses, and he whipped off the tablecloth and draped it over Davey's unconscious body.

"Right, let's go and talk to Roebuck," Grant said decisively.

Chapter Twenty-Nine

Mary knew the way to Roebuck's study, naturally. She led them through the great hall, where Felicity Roebuck was talking to small groups and the party was in full swing. It had been billed as a business networking evening and charity auction. The charities were a local children's hospice, a local woman's refuge and the Red Crescent's campaign to help people in Syria. Grant struggled not to find any irony in the choices but supposed Felicity Roebuck was organising this night and he had no reason to believe she was involved in anything untoward.

A wood-panelled corridor led off the far end of the great hall and the entire length was lined with paintings of the estate and various portraits of its former keepers. Roebuck was old money and the manor had been rebuilt in the Georgian years after being ravaged by fire. Mary was full of facts and Grant guessed that when she was with Roebuck, she had been genuinely in love. She hesitated at the door. It was a double oak door over eight-feet high.

"It's okay, I'll go in," Grant said. "You wait here."

She looked a little relieved, but said, "I want to see his face. I want to see what he has to say."

"No. I don't want it getting emotional. This needs to be done calmly."

"Like you did with that rodent Keith Davey?"

Grant shrugged. "Nevertheless, give me the chance to get through to him."

He didn't bother to knock, simply pushed the right-hand door. It moved inwards and he saw Roebuck sat at a large, curved desk some twenty feet in front of him. The polish was high, the wood dark. Grant thought it to be mahogany, but he knew for sure that it hadn't come from *Ikea*. Nor had the collection of shotguns on the wall behind him. Each one was secured with a lockable clamp through the trigger guard. There would have to have been fifty of them spread into a fan. A whole semi-circle, a half-moon of exquisitely engraved metal and highly polished walnut, barrels of blue, black, stainless steel and the brown patina of Damascus steel.

"You like?" Roebuck turned and looked at the collection.

"They're better on the wall than pointed at somebody, I suppose."

Roebuck chuckled. "Some of them are worth a quarter of a million, perhaps a little more. Holland and Holland and the odd Purdy mainly. English only, nothing foreign." He smiled as he turned back and looked at him. "So, DCI Grant, how can I help you?"

"I think you know," he ventured.

"I know Bunt is up to something," Roebuck said. "But I don't know what. That rat-like creature Keith Davey too."

"Then why haven't you tried to find out?"

"I've rather blotted my copybook, so it would seem."

"Meaning?"

Roebuck leaned back in his chair, held up his hands in a gesture of accepting a mistake. "I haven't been whiter than white in business. Some of my dealings have left me compromised, to say the least."

"How so? Start with Davey." Grant stood a few feet from the desk. He didn't look for a chair, his stance was dominant, and he wanted to keep the man off balance.

"I haven't declared my interest in Keith and Davey. I'm in for a huge sum of VAT and tax. We also skirted a few planning issues and bribed some of Cornwall's more suscep-tible planning officers and parish councillors. Not merely a bung, more like a bloody fortune."

"But that would affect Davey."

"When I say we..."

"Davey will claim he knows nothing?"

"I rather showed off at first," Roebuck shook his head. "Bloody stupid, I know. We shared the same lawyer, he introduced us."

"John Pascoe?"

"Yes! How did you know?"

"I know things. Go on."

"I'm up to my bloody eyeballs in corruption. Davey knows it, so we continue to buy out the people no longer able to live on their own. I use the places in my care homes as part of their payment. Davey has off-set profits and bought his way into most of my residential homes."

Grant nodded thoughtfully, then asked, "Is there a correlation between deaths in your homes and you buying them out? A higher percentage of residents dying who have released their equity as a care package?"

"Oh Jesus..." Roebuck put his elbows on the desk,

bowed his head into his hands. "I can check. I never thought..."

Grant nodded. "What about the sex trade?"

"The what?" Roebuck looked up, his expression one of confusion.

"You know about Mary Hocking's mother, don't you?"

"Look, my wife went bloody ape-shit when she heard I had been cheating on her again. There would be no second chances, and she has the majority share in the manor, so what could I do? I ended it but kept Mary's mother in The Richmond. I felt I owed her *something* from our affair." Roebuck held his hands up again. "What's this about the sex trade?"

"I think, or rather I know, that Keith Davey and your solicitor, John Pascoe are running prostitutes out of vacant properties throughout Cornwall."

"What?"

"Mary has been forced into the sex trade to keep her mother in luxury living at your care home, but it has been more than merely hinted at by Pascoe that harm would come to her mother if she did not do as she was told..."

"Oh, my poor dear..." Roebuck shook his head, his eyes looked teary, and his lips trembled slightly. "The bastards! I never knew, I swear."

"So, what has Bunt got on you?"

Roebuck scoffed, then sighed. "I have allowed that man too much freedom. I have used him in the past as a..." he hesitated.

"An enforcer?"

"Sort of," Roebuck sighed. "He was a strong arm in some tough times. I have had many facets to my business dealings. Bunt was a constant companion, and I confided in him from time to time. The man just had a nasty little habit of remembering everything. I know he is in with Keith Davey and John Pascoe. I just don't know what."

"I think I do," Grant said. "Tell me, why did you take that shot at us?"

"It was Bunt."

"But *you* had the rifle."

"I took it from him. We were looking for an injured buck. A poacher took a shot at it and left the beast injured. Blew most of its snout off. Now it can't eat or drink. Who the hell takes a head shot at a bloody deer?" Grant shrugged. He had no idea, but guessed it was a no-no. "Bunt carried my rifle on the shoulder sling. He had his shotgun with him to pop a couple of pigeons afterwards. We never found the buck. Bunt saw you and took a shot. He was trying to scare you off. He takes his role as gamekeeper a little too seriously. He got off another before I managed to snatch the rifle off him, gave him a bollocking, for what it's worth, and came down to talk to you."

"It felt like *you* were warning us off."

"You were with that female detective sergeant. I've had a few dealings with her, don't care for her much. No leeway. By the book and be damned with it. That's not how it should work down here. There should be some leeway, a slap on the wrist, no harm done. She's in it for promotions. Ladder climber, that one."

"What were those enquiries for?"

Roebuck shrugged. "Farm labourers. We had a lot of Polish, and they're great workers. Bloody Brexit ruined that. But we also had some Romanians and Albanians working the farms, and they were quite a savage bunch. They fought, fucked and stole everything they could. And they weren't strictly legal, either."

"You mean illegal," Grant stated.

"You're as bad as she is," Roebuck chided. He saw the seriousness of Grant's expression, then added, "Bunt oversees that aspect, the casual labour. The estate owns over twenty-thousand acres throughout the Duchy. We grow daffodils and vegetables mainly. That requires labour and lots of it, but on a casual basis."

Grant nodded. "Do you know about the smuggling cave, or tunnel near where you saw us near the creek?"

"Of course!"

"When did you lock it up?"

Roebuck pondered. "I suppose, ten years ago. Maybe a dozen years. We had some kids from over on the point discover it. They turned it into a sort of den. It was innocent at first, swallows and amazons' stuff, but then a year or two later it was all fags and booze, then drugs and sex... It got to the point that they were practically holding raves in there. I had it sealed and bolted because some of the parents said I was encouraging illicit behaviour. I had some workers patrol around so that they got the message."

"Well, it's been in use recently," Grant said. "The hinges are well oiled, the padlocks look new to me, and there's signs of the ground being walked on."

"Bunt has something to hide. That's why he took the shots. Nothing's going to halt someone's progress like a couple of three-oh-eight bullets at their feet." Roebuck reached for a tumbler and the decanter of amber liquid. Grant supposed it was brandy. It seemed like the drink to have in one's study. "I take it you won't be joining me?" He smiled as Grant shook his head. "If I know Bunt, it'll be alcohol and tobacco. Cigarettes without the duty. Marvellous, all I need is attention from HM Revenue and Customs. What with my aversion to VAT and taxes..."

"I'll stop you there..." Grant interrupted. "I have reason to believe that Pete Bunt has brought illegal immigrants into the country, using your smuggling cave as a place to imprison them, culminating in them being exploited in either modern-day slavery on your farms or forced into the sex slave trade..."

"He wouldn't!" Roebuck blurted. He stared at Grant for a moment, then shook his head and picked up his drink. He swilled the contents down, drained them in one gulp. He screwed up his face as the liquid burned its way down. "Oh, for God's sake..."

"You know it wouldn't be a stretch of the imagination, don't you?"

He nodded, though somewhat reluctantly. "And you think Keith Davey and John Pascoe are involved as well?"

"It would appear so," answered Grant.

Roebuck seemed to flop in his chair, like the stuffing had been knocked out of him. "Then I'm bloody doomed," he said. "It will all come out... The police and HMRC will look into all my dealings..."

Grant nodded. "Oh, they certainly will. But you deserve it. You deserve to be investigated, you deserve to be fined, to have your properties seized and go to prison for a long, long time." Grant turned and walked to the door. He looked back at the man behind the desk. He was a shadow of his former self, broken. "You almost had me. I almost felt you were okay. I mean, a posh twat with a dodgy past and a certain flair for skirting the law, but okay, nonetheless. But you never thought to ask who Bunt trafficked, or how many people. You never thought to ask from where, nor what has become of them. You and Bunt are two peas in a pod. One has money and privilege, the other has come from nowhere, but I'm sure he has accumulated a great deal from other people's misery. You both have. You, Bunt, Davey and Pascoe are all one in the same. They just moved on without you, left the deadwood behind so to speak." Grant opened the door and left. Roebuck said nothing and remained motionless behind the desk, staring at the floor.

Chapter Thirty

Grant took out his iPhone and switched off the recording function. He readied it again and slipped it back into his pocket. Two for two. Both Davey's and Roebuck's confessions. He suspected that neither would be permissible in court, but difficult to ignore, especially depending on how the evidence was either used or leaked. He looked for Mary on his way out. He checked the corridor and the great hall. The gathering was in full swing, and the sound was of chatter and clinking glasses, punctuated by hoots of laughter, some sincere, some not. He walked on, checked the self-service bar. There were people in here, but this room was quieter. Business talk, or assignations. A room where privacy had been sought away from the boisterousness of the main event. He couldn't see any sign of Mary, and in her red dress with flowing red hair around her shoulders, she would be difficult to miss. He checked beside the bar but noticed that Davey had gone. He would have come round with a headache and a little worse for wear. But they had been clean punches, bruising and a split lip. The money shot had been delivered to the point of the man's chin. A real *lights-out* punch, but no broken teeth or shattered eye sockets. He knew the man would not be making an official complaint. There was too much for him to lose. Keith Davey was in as deep as he could get.

Felicity Roebuck was no longer taking the tickets, the night was in full swing, and it looked like the great and the good were in attendance. The table was empty, except for an arrangement of gift bags which had been put out after the last guests had been admitted. Grant had paid a total of four-hundred pounds for both his and Mary's tickets, so he swiped two of the bags on the way out. He glanced inside as he walked down the steps and across the gravelled drive-way. The spotlights pointed on the house gave enough ambient light for him to see by, and he saw vouchers for spa days, a selection of locally made chocolates, a voucher for a meal at a local restaurant and some sort of scented candle with a sticker of a tin mine on the base, so he guessed this was some sort of advertising loss-leader for a local candle maker. He was sure that Mary would enjoy both bags. They reminded him of children's party bags. His wife had always had them waiting for her guests as they left Chloe's birthday parties. He smiled. In his day it had been a slice of cake and a balloon if you were lucky.

When he reached his car, he opened the boot and put the two bags into the cubby, then took out the torch and a pair of heavy-duty bolt-croppers that had set him back eighty-pounds from a local hardware and home store chain. Among other things, he had bought a sixteen-ounce claw hammer as well. He wasn't a practical man, in that he lived in a rented apartment in London and seldom needed to do DIY, but he figured he knew the fundamentals to getting those wrought iron gates open. He set out across the lawn to the side of the house, switched on the beam of the torch and shone it out across the rear lawns. He saw the ground slope down beyond and saw lights in the distance, which he took to be the various villages and hamlets on the point. Downhill was the right direction, so he strode out, keeping the beam on its lowest setting to avoid being too conspicuous. The torch was an internet special he had owned for several years, a SWAT/special forces model that claimed to be the most powerful hand-held model on the market. Whether that was true or not, he knew he hadn't seen many brighter.

A barrier of stock fencing separated the lawns from the open field. It was a three-rung iron fence around five-feet high and designed to keep the deer or farm animals off the two-tone striped lawn. He climbed over and dropped lightly onto the ground. He instantly felt the unevenness of the ground underfoot, the grass was longer as well. The terrain became rougher and steeper, and he started to slip on early dew forming on the grass, his shoes were more suited to bars and great halls than to rambling. He turned the torch on and twisted the aperture to get a narrower, but more concentrated beam. The light shone powerfully out to three-hundred metres and on the edge of that lay the woodland he could see from the other side of the creek.

After ten minutes, Grant reached the fringe of the woods and switched off the torch. He remained still for a good five minutes, taking in his surroundings and listening for the night sounds. His ears became more accustomed, as did his eyes, but he would need the torch again in a moment and that would render his night vision useless once more. He could pick out the sound of early fallen leaves rustling on the ground, the noise of small rodents or perhaps a fox breaking through the undergrowth. The occasional screeches, he put down to owls or foxes, he wasn't sure which. But he did know that in the countryside at night, there was always sounds of the hunters and the hunted. The food chain in constant motion.

When he switched the torch on again using the low-power setting and widening the beam. He also kept it low, searching the ground in front of him for the huge granite boulders that would tell him he was near. The woods looked different at night, and from this approach, he wasn't sure he was on track. He could see lights across the river, this time he figured, or at least hoped, it was Loe Creek. This meant he was also nearing the other end of the woods. He swept the torch in wider arcs, switched up the power and closed the width of the beam down. He caught sight of the first granite boulder, the size of a small hatchback, and looked down for the trail. After a few minutes he was on it and he turned around and headed back up hill, following the trail around on a loose parallel with the creek. He made his way through the boulders, feeling a little uneasy at being hemmed in, and thoroughly relieved when he came out into the opening and saw the entrance to the cave.

He played the light on the gates, took advantage of illuminating the entire mouth of the cave, but noticed it veered sharply to the left. He used the bolt-croppers to snap the hasp of the padlock, surprised at how easy it had been. The bolt-croppers were pneumatic, giving tension a hundred times what Grant could have mustered alone. He threaded the chain through the bars and let them drop to the dry earth. There was no needed for the hammer, which he had tucked into his waistband, but he did not know whether he would need the bolt-croppers again, so kept them with him as he set off down the tunnel.

Chapter Thirty-One

Grant could hear them before he saw them. There was the sound of muffled voices and crying. But it was more than that. There was an air of misery. He couldn't think what it was, but as he rounded another bend in the tunnel, which had been gradually tapering smaller in overall dimension, he could *feel* the depression in the atmosphere.

The walls of the tunnel were a mixture of solid rock with pick-marks and drill holes where dynamite or black powder charges would once have been used to cut through the rock. In places the tunnel was boarded with rotten-looking planks. Sure enough, in these areas, a fine dust of rock debris and dried soil rained between the planks lining the ceiling. Just a fine and occasional sprinkling, like shaking icing sugar over a cake. Grant looked at the ceiling ominously. Ahead of him the roof had been haphazardly propped with four-by-four posts. These looked more like rotten wood than freshly milled timber. This section of the tunnel was some two-feet lower than the previous section and looked to have sunk over time. At just over six-feet tall, he came close to scraping his head on the rafters.

He played the beam across the walls and ceiling, hesitated when he saw the build-up of debris on the floor, but the voices spurred him onwards. He could hear the suffering, the fear, the uncertainty. He was no fan of enclosed spaces, had suffered and panicked in the boot of his own car, but he needed to keep moving forwards.

Grant spread the beam of the torch so that it illuminated the entire tunnel in front and to each side of him. The light was brilliant white. It turned the tunnel into daylight, but when he glanced over his shoulder, the tunnel was a black hole of total darkness. He decided right there and then that he would not add caving to his bucket list of activities. He could hear more voices now, and as he rounded the next bend he could see movement ahead. The voices ceased and there was a sense of panic in the air. Hushed tones, quickly spoken sentences which sounded rushed and reciprocated. Another few paces and the light picked out bars on both sides of the tunnel where recesses had been dug or blasted out of the rock. These would have been stores for rum and tobacco and other goods brought in to avoid the customs officers over two-hundred years ago. A time when Trenvarth Manor would have been more than just a businessman's residence, but the centre of commerce and employment to the surrounding villages. This cave and stores would have either been constructed right under the Lord of the Manor's nose without his knowledge, by the very workers he employed, or was perhaps the reason for the manor owner's increasing wealth. A secret venture to keep the locals onside and in cheap alcohol and tobacco. Grant would hazard a guess that this storage cavern was indeed directly under the manor house itself. In which case, there was most likely a route into the manor, if it hadn't been sealed at some point over the years. Otherwise, there seemed little point in excavating so far. Grant suspected that previous squires of Trenvarth Manor had profited greatly from smuggled bounty.

Grant shone the torch around him, but there was no bounty in these dugouts. Not unless you counted humans as commodity. He lowered the torch from the blinking faces and switched to the lowest power setting. Three women, Grant guessed to be anywhere from their late-teens to their early-twenties, stood at the bars to the cell on his right. He looked at the cell to his left. A man and a woman stood huddled together. They were attempting to shield a child of around nine or ten. Grant couldn't see for sure, but he'd bet anything that it was a little girl. The same little girl who had lost her teddy bear three nights earlier.

"I'm here to help," he said quietly, slowly. "Does anybody speak English?"

The man nodded. "Little Engleesh..." he replied even more slowly. "I am Abdul..."

"I speak English. Who are you?" a voice behind echoed out confidently from the other cell.

Grant turned around, saw one of the young women standing slightly further forward than the other two. He raised the torch, not intrusively, just enough to highlight her features. He could see dried blood on her face, her clothes filthy and ripped. There was an overwhelming fetid smell, an overpowering stench of both sweat and urine and faeces. It reminded Grant of a trip he once had with Chloe to the zoo on a hot day. In the domestic farmyard petting enclosure where they could stroke and pat the goats. He tried not to wrinkle his nose. He could see that the women had used a corner of their cell as a toilet. Near the bars, on the other side of the cell, cases of bottled water and an outer box of ready to eat camping/trekking meals in foil bags had been broken into, empty packets lay strewn next to the box. There were candles burning, but he hadn't noticed them at first due to the power of his torch. It was a medieval prison. Horrifyingly basic and would have been terrifying in the silent darkness of the tunnel.

"I am a policeman, a detective. I am a senior ranking officer," he said reassuringly. "My name is Grant. You can call all me..."

"I'll call you Mohammed, Buddha or Jesus Christ almighty if you get us the hell out of here..." she said sharply. Her accent was middle east meets the Kardashians and she had a spark in her eye and a look of defiance on her face. She looked at the bolt-croppers in his hand. "Are you going to use those, or what?"

Grant snapped to and searched for the padlock on the chain securing the cell bars. He put the handle of the torch in his mouth and used both hands to operate the bolt-croppers. This padlock was stronger than the one securing the entrance and Grant had to take several attempts, but eventually it pinged off and the chain separated, and the women stepped forwards together and grabbed the bars. Grant pulled and they pushed, and the bars opened. Two of the women rushed across the tunnel and flung themselves at the bars of the other cell. There were kisses and hugging, as best they could and the woman who had done the talking hugged Grant in a way he'd never felt before. A total and complete show of gratitude with a sincerity he was barely able to comprehend. She let go and joined the others, who were by now looking expectantly at him to get the padlock off. He wasted no more time, worked on the bolt and had it cut cleanly within a minute. The man pushed the door out and hugged the three young women, his eyes closed as he savoured every particle of them, as if every second of the moment was regaining an hour stolen from him. The man turned and hugged Grant and he dropped the bolt-croppers, taken by surprise and shaken at the power of the hug. He tapped the man on the back and the man released him, his wife was already in an embrace with her four daughters.

"Thank you, thank you," the man said.

Grant was about to tell him it was alright, but the sudden illumination of the cavern startled him, and everyone else. The torch was bright, but the complete white light from the half-dozen one-hundred-watt bulbs that flicked on overhead was incomparable. He looked around him, noted that the cavern was indeed the end of the line. The rest of the tunnel was sealed with concrete blocks and mortar. They had been cut neatly into the curvature of the tunnel walls. He watched the tunnel, a sense of foreboding and indecision upon him all at once.

Keith Davey rounded the bend, and he carried a shotgun. Ornate and shining in the bright light. Grant wondered if Roebuck's display fan of shotguns on the wall had a missing space. As the man neared, Grant could see he had bound his middle finger to his ring finger with a makeshift bandage of what looked like a strip of linen napkin. It made the way he held the weapon look somewhat awkward, but his trigger finger was unaffected and wrapped around the forward trigger.

"Oh, isn't that touching..." he said, smiling. "A family reunion. Well, it won't last long. There are plans for this lot."

Grant stared at him as he approached. He shook his head. "Like the others?"

"Hopefully not," he said. "They were quite a handful, the *Hafeez's*, or whatever the hell they were called..."

"Qasim, a doctor. Yara also a doctor," Grant paused. "Shabnam and Amira aged nineteen, Fatma aged seventeen and Gita aged fifteen...." he spat at him. "And you killed them. You could at least remember their names..."

Davey shook his head. "I didn't kill anyone... That was Pascoe and Bunt. But the trouble was, I don't think we softened them up enough before putting them to work," he added.

"Meaning? Is this what this is about?" he asked, waving a hand towards the cell. "Dehumanising them? Making them want more and appreciating it when they get it?"

"Sort of," Davey smiled. "These girls will be pleased for a hot meal, a shower and some clean clothes. Having to fuck a dozen different men a day won't seem such a hardship when they know how tough things can be."

Grant shook his head. "You are all idiots. I don't know about these people, but the Hafeez family endured years of hardship in Syria. Little food, no clean water, hardly any medical attention. No heating in the harsh winters and no respite in the hot, dusty summers. Then they set out to trek across Turkey and Europe to get here. Month upon month on the trail, roads and in the back of lorries. They only *knew* hardship. That's why you couldn't break them down."

"No, they were a handful alright. But we've learned. The woman was a good fuck, she got the message. She seemed to catch on to what was best for her family. But the husband..." he shrugged. "We just couldn't get through to him."

"And..." Grant wasn't sure he wanted the answer, but he asked anyway. It was the detective in him. "...the children?"

"Hardly children." Davey shrugged. "But we had plenty of bidders. A bit of a ring going on. There's plenty of people who want what the heart desires... But you've got to keep them in line. The punters, that is. They tend to talk, invite friends in on it. Well, we closed it all down to re-evaluate how best to go forward."

"So, you drowned them?" Grant spat at him.

He shrugged. "Bunt did it. He killed them all. Easy enough. A noose on a pole. Take them down a few feet under the surface and wait. They soon stop their struggling. Mind you, the others didn't much like having to watch and knowing that they would be next..."

"Bastards!" the woman who had done the talking screamed. She started to translate hurriedly to the rest of her family. The man and his wife looked horrified, pulled their off-spring closer.

"Yeah, well," Davey stared at them. "At least you know what's coming if you don't cooperate." He walked a few feet closer, aimed the shotgun at the group. "And that goes for every one of you camel-fuckers!"

Grant shook his head. "You thought the DNA from all of the people who abused them sexually would be lost in the seawater, didn't you?"

Davey sneered. "But it wouldn't be. Not for sure. Hundreds of mineshafts to lose them down, never see them again, and Bunt opted for drowning them. He and John Pascoe thought making them look like asylum-seekers who capsized and drowned would work better. But Pascoe's police contact said that the DNA would hold up to an autopsy. Everyone sweated for a while, but they ended up buried in Swanvale without a post-mortem. We could thank the local Muslim community for that."

"But you thought you'd get them dug up and disposed

of in case an exhumation and autopsy were ever sought at a later date?" Grant stared at Davey. "Down that mineshaft you mentioned, I suppose." He paused. "But Bunt was seen and that's why he drowned John Trevithick in the same manner."

"Shame, that one," Davey paused. "Bunt knew him for years. Not a bad bloke, by all accounts."

Grant still held the torch in his right hand, down by his side. He had been working the aperture carefully in his hand, tightening the beam. The cavern was well lit, but the tactical torch was equipped with a strobe, emitting twice the light of the beam, around a million candlepower, and flashing ten times a second. Davey was six feet away, but the shotgun looked steady in his hands. He imagined the man taking a peg at the pheasant drive and blasting a hundred or more of the poor birds from the sky during a brandy-fuelled day with Roebuck and their business associates. He had no reason to believe the man was anything other than an expert shot with the weapon.

"Right," Davey said decisively. "Get back in the cells." He looked at Grant and smiled, adding, "You as well, detective."

The woman who had done the talking suddenly screeched like a banshee and bolted forwards. The woman had guts. Davey swung the shotgun at the same time as Grant pressed the strobe button and the light disco-balled in Davey's eyes. He squinted, held a hand to his eyes and swung the weapon one handed. The noise of the shotgun blast was deafening in the confines of the cavern. There were simultaneous screams from the women, and the husband went down. He had been skimmed by a few pellets, but those pellets had been at point-blank range and his shirt had turned crimson at his right shoulder. Grant grabbed the barrel with his left hand and felt the searing heat in his palm as he pushed the barrel out from him and straightened his arm rigidly. He turned to the family and screamed for them to run. They didn't need telling twice, and they pulled their father to his feet, the mother swept up the youngest daughter and they were on their feet like greyhounds out of the gate.

Davey kicked out, but it was weak, and he was off-balance. Grant kicked back and drove the ball of his foot into the man's gut. He fell backwards, but kept hold of the shotgun, trying desperately to bring it around onto Grant. He was determined, knew he was out of options, and this would be the last fight he'd have. Grant knew it, too. But he'd been in this position before, and he knew how far he could go. He threw the torch into Davey's face and the man yelped as it smashed into his eye. It was enough for him to release his grip on the shotgun, and it dropped with a clatter onto the ground, Grant letting go of his grip on the barrels to keep a hold on his opponent. Davey punched and flailed, but he was not a strong man. Grant caught hold of him, positioned him well, then pounded him in his already bruised face. He went down hard, a repeat of the incident at the bar, but he landed right next to the shotgun and went for it. Grant calculated the distance, but he knew he'd never make it and was already running. He swept up the torch, which was still strobing and reached the end of the cavern as the shotgun blast echoed out. He didn't feel its blast, but he heard the pellets as they clattered and ricocheted off the rock walls. He could hear the man opening the breach and reloading the barrels behind him. The tunnel was long and before the next corner, Davey would hit him for sure. He grabbed the brand-new claw hammer out from his waistband, and as he raced past the low section of ceiling, he smashed the hammer against the first of the four by four post. It rocked out and debris dropped from the ceiling. Grant hit the next one, and the next. He could hear the posts clattering on the rock floor behind him, the sound of twenty pounds of dirt hitting the ground each time. Without losing momentum, he knocked out the last post and the sound behind him was deafening. The roof of the tunnel dropped with hundreds of tonnes of rock and soil falling all at once. The lights running down the tunnel went off and turned Grant's world into darkness, interspersed with the strobing of brilliant white light. He was lifted off his feet by a great wind, the force of the rock-fall behind him, and it carried him a clear twenty-feet down into the darkness. He landed in a heap, his face in the dirt. He had dropped the torch, but it was impossible to lose. When he reached it, he switched off the strobe and widened the beam. The cave was entirely blocked with earth and rocks, some as large as household appliances, several tonnes in weight. He heard a sound and turned around sharply. It was the young woman who had done the talking.

"Are you okay?" she asked tentatively.

"I think so," he replied. "Where are your family?"

She shrugged. "I thought I would come back to help you," she said. "You helped us out of there... It was the least I could do."

Chapter Thirty-Two

G rant had noticed the strobing of the blue lights, recognised the play of illumination off the walls of the building from countless crime scenes nearing fifteen years of service. He didn't know if the family had noticed. They were huddled tightly and talking in their own language. Grant knew they were safe now and had relayed this to the young woman. She had spoken to the rest of her family, and the look of relief on their faces was insurmountable.

There were three police vehicles and two ambulances. All had their blue lights operating on top. Grant surveyed the scene, watched as the uniformed officers bunched the guests into a sort of holding area, while plain clothed detectives prepared clipboards for interviewing. Grant frowned but walked on with the family behind him. He saw DS Clark and she hurried over.

"Jesus! What happened to you?" she asked. She looked at the bedraggled family and frowned at him. "Who are these people?" Grant stared at her, but she raised her eyebrows in annoyance. "I'm sorry about yesterday, you saw my note, right?"

"What note?" He thought about the house, the room for clients, the hit on the back of his head, the boot of the car, the clifftop, the fight... "What are you talking about?"

"I got an urgent call," she said. "You were upstairs in the loo, I felt a little embarrassed at calling up to you, to speak to you through the bathroom door... I left a note on the kitchen table along with your coffee." She paused. "Warleggan told me about your letter. What the hell were you thinking? You couldn't possibly have hoped to get away with it, acting unofficially. I didn't let on that I'd seen you..."

"And where did you see me?"

She frowned, reached out and touched his shoulder tenderly. "Are you okay, Grant?" "Of course," he said. "Where were we? Whose house was that? Yours?"

"No!" she replied hostilely. "I never said it was my house. It was a place in one of our investigations. I borrowed the keys, that's all. I wanted somewhere safe to talk. Hey, don't mention it, okay? I'll get into serious trouble." Grant nodded and she said, "Look, we'll talk later. I have work to do."

"What's happened?"

"Claude Roebuck," she said. "He turned a shotgun on himself in the middle of his charity gala."

"Where?"

"In his study," she said. "His wife discovered the body. She went looking for him. Seems an ex-lover of his was here tonight, bold as brass. She thought he was up to his old tricks and thought she'd catch him out. Then she found him..." She turned and started back towards the house.

He called out, "Do you know a man called John Pascoe?"

She stopped and looked back, frowning. "Lawyer. Slimy bloke." She nodded. "Yeah, our paths have crossed. He's a lawyer who turns a blind eye to stuff. His family are well respected, but they're wealthy. But they didn't get that way by being nice."

"How so?"

"They own property, hotels and holiday lets. They get the planning they need and don't pay all the VAT or tax they should. Keep their staff on either zero-hour contracts or training schemes that have them working illegal hours for half the minimum wage, or so I hear," she paused. "Big in the freemasons too. Funny handshakes, rolled-up trouser legs and back-scratching. Well, they all are, aren't they?"

"Who?"

"The ones who get on down here. Those, and the ones who *want* to get on." She turned and walked back to the steps, jogged up them and disappeared inside.

Grant waved at a uniformed officer, beckoning the man to come over. He did so, a little begrudgingly. Grant explained what had happened, that the family had been imprisoned. He asked if he could get them some water first, then contact a senior officer. He wanted to keep it out of the hands of CID for a moment, see them properly entered into the system before he did what he planned next. He watched the officer walk up the steps to the house. It looked like he spoke to a waiter hovering at the top of the steps and he too walked inside. Less than a minute later, DCI Warleggan came out and stood at the top of the steps. He surveyed the area, then made his way down the steps and walked towards them. Grant groaned inwardly. He backed away from the family, took out his iPhone and took a picture of all of them, huddled in their group. He thumbed the screen, then looked at Warleggan as he drew near. When he looked up DS Chris Jago was approaching from another direction. The light shone off his red hair and it made his greying beard appear whiter. He looked like Santa Clause for a moment, and the sight was surreal.

"What are you doing?" the DCI asked incredulously.

"I've just taken a picture of these people, and emailed it, along with a short report, to

Devon and Cornwall HQ in Exeter. I have also uploaded it to the internal server at Scotland

Yard."

"You don't trust me?"

"I don't trust anyone I meet down here," Grant paused, eyed DS Jago for a moment. "These people have just become public knowledge. They have entered the system. I'm handing them over to you now, DS Jago."

"Where did you find them?" Jago asked.

"They were being held in cells built in an old smuggling tunnel on the creek side of the estate." Grant watched the uniformed officer return with two waiters. One carried a tray full of glasses of water and orange juice, the other carried a large selection of canapés. It looked comical, given the state of the family's appearance, but they did not waste time tucking in. Grant said, "There was a cave-in. A section of the roof of the tunnel collapsed. Lucky timing, I guess."

DS Jago nodded towards the family. "So, what's their story?"

"Refugees. Syrian I'd bet," Grant paused, took his iPhone back out of his pocket. "I've got Claude Roebuck's insight into what Pete Bunt, Keith Davey and John Pascoe were up to..."

"Pascoe?" Warleggan asked. "The solicitor?"

"The same."

"Are you sure?" DS Jago asked. He looked at Warleggan, then back to Grant. "There's all sorts of ramifications if that's the case..."

Warleggan moved it on. He looked like he was pressed for time and the Syrian family was another hassle he didn't need. "What were they up to?"

"I've got Davey's confession on here too."

"Give it to me."

"No," Grant said. "When I get a better signal or onto some Wi-Fi, I'll upload it. Same as before. Exeter and Scotland Yard first."

"I could take it. It's evidence."

"You could try. I wouldn't recommend it."

Warleggan shook his head. "You think you're a real hot shot, don't you?" He shrugged. "Alright, what is Davey's confession. The salient facts, I've got a shit storm here."

"What's going on?" Grant asked.

"You first."

Grant shrugged. "Davey, Bunt and Pascoe ran a sex ring together. From what I gather it ran through from straight to gay to paedophilia. But the straight aspect would still have been nothing more than rape. I don't even know how to begin classifying the rest of it," Grant nodded towards the family, now enjoying smoked salmon and caviar on blinis. They must have been thinking this was how the English ate every day. "These people were lucky. If you can believe that. They were brought in by boat three nights ago. The night that I was assaulted, and you did nothing about it..." Warleggan seemed to be taking it on board. He nodded, remained silent. "Bunt and Pascoe saw me watching them." Grant looked towards the house and the gathering of guests. "So, your turn. What's happening here?"

Warleggan stared at him. "Claude Roebuck is dead."

"He killed himself?"

"No. Why would he?"

"Listen to the recording later."

"Well, he didn't kill himself. But he was shot with one of his own shotguns. Know anything about that?"

"You suspect me?"

"Well, you turned up here tonight with his mistress in tow. And you both headed towards his study. It's not a stretch of the imagination."

Grant laughed. "Not for your limited imagination, no."

"Meaning?" Warleggan snapped.

"Davey turned up in the cave with a shotgun. Ornate and expensive, by the look of it."

"And?"

"And he held us at gunpoint. We all escaped, I fought with him and managed to get away. The last I know of him, he was shooting at me and missed. He hit a strut, the roof caved in and about ten tonnes of rock and earth ended up on his head."

"Shit! He's still in there?"

"He isn't going anywhere..." Grant paused. "When he's eventually dug out, you'll find the shotgun. I don't think you'll have any problem matching the lead shot in the cartridges with what's inside Roebuck's body. The male refugee, as well for that matter."

Warleggan turned and took out his mobile phone and started to dial as he walked away towards the house. It was turning into a busy night for him.

Grant looked at DS Chris Jago. "Right, now he's gone, I want to talk to you."

The detective nodded. "Okay..." he said somewhat uneasily.

"Bunt and Pascoe dug up the Hafeez family because somebody convinced them that DNA would be an issue if they were exhumed, and a proper autopsy was ever sought. That somebody was a local police officer."

"You suspect the DCI?" he asked incredulously.

"You called for further action in the investigation. It was denied by Warleggan. I trust you." He opened his iPhone and thumbed down to his contacts. "What's your email address?" Jago told him and Grant typed it in. "I'm sending you the recordings of both Roebuck and Davey, both made tonight. You need to get a search out for Pete Bunt too. He's a priority and with a fishing boat, he has the means to get away, head in any direction and stay off the radar."

"I'll get on it." He looked at the family, now eating what looked like soft-poached quail's egg wrapped in pancetta. "I'll call social services right now and get them accommodation for the night. They look in rough shape. They'll get clean clothes and a shower."

"They're crucial witnesses. They will identify Pete Bunt and John Pascoe as their abductors."

"John Pascoe has been listed as a missing person. It's early, but he had appointments he didn't keep and that's out of character."

Grant thought back to the clifftop, the axe, his battered body on the ground... "Maybe he caught wind of all this and has taken off," he suggested.

"Most likely, by the sounds of it," he said. "I'll get the ball rolling here," he said and turned towards the family.

Grant made his way towards the house. He needed to find Mary and tell her what had transpired. But most of all, he wanted to warn her that the link left in the chain, Pete Bunt, was on the run and had nothing to lose.

Chapter Thirty-Three

*D*ay one...
Grant awoke, ripped from his stupor by the incessant banging. Metal on metal, absorbed and echoed by wood. Heavy oak, but even that seemed to be shaking within the frame.

He should have tipped Maitland's Scotch down the sink when he had arrived, should have washed it down the drain along with the wine and the beer. But he'd washed the filthy liquid down his own throat instead. He had kidded himself that he could stop at one, but the devil on his shoulder dug in his claws and accepted another. And then the deal was done, he'd signed up again and drank the place dry.

He could have coped without the drink had he not continued to recount the last moments of the Hafeez family in his mind. The gaps had been filled and the horror of the reality would not leave him alone. The image of them scared and knowing their fate, watching their loved ones taken one by one and drowned in such a cold and proficient fashion. Who had been first? Who had been the lucky one? Who had endured the torturous scene for the duration?

Who had watched the other five members taken one by one and pushed under kicking and screaming, pulled out lifeless and still? Grant thought of them, used and abused, terrified and aware at the end, knowing their time had come, that they would never gaze upon their family again or take in another day. Something so casual about the way Keith Davey had regaled the facts. Those people had been nothing more than a commodity in a market almost too sick to imagine, yet alone witness. The family that Grant saved from the cave would have suffered a similar fate, because as much as they would try to break them, the human body and spirit has untold resolves, and he could see it in their eyes that they would have kept on fighting. How long before they too would have been drowned out at sea because they did not break? Or thrown down that ominous mineshaft; one of so many hidden and overgrown shafts that littered the county? Grant could see the futility in life. There wasn't always someone who could help. There were countless people out there suffering even worse fates and meeting similar ends. The thoughts of this, over and over throughout the night had made him reach for a bottle. And then another. Now came the regret. Now came the knowledge that the agony of over sixty days of staying dry had been in vain. That he had broken over sixty promises to himself, but ultimately, he had broken the promise he had made to Chloe. She would never know, he would never tell her, but *he* would know every second of every day that he had let her down, too. Today was the first day. And today would be the hardest day of all.

The banging hadn't stopped. He had double locked and bolted every door, feeling vulnerable that Pete Bunt was still at large. He had uploaded the recordings to DS Jago and to Middlemoor, the headquarters of the Devon and

Cornwall police in Exeter. He had also sent the file to the internal server at his office at Scotland Yard. He had sent the photographs of the family to each address as well. This family, whoever they were, were now in the system and accounted for. no amount of corruption could lose them. He could do no more for them.

He swung his legs off the sofa and stood up unsteadily. He had slept in his clothes. Now the shirt and trousers looked creased and twisted. He straightened them the best he could and headed towards the front door. The banging was both loud and impatient. He pulled back the bolt and turned the key, then opened the door inwards and blinked at the intrusive daylight.

"Took your time," DCI Warleggan said curtly.

Grant looked at him but said nothing. He looked at DS Clark standing beside him. His mouth feeling like wool. He had no saliva, and he knew he looked a state. "What's wrong?"

"Where were you between ten o'clock last-night and five this morning?" Warleggan asked accusingly.

"Why?"

"Answer the question."

"Am I under arrest?"

"No."

"Then stick your question."

"You're not under arrest, yet." Warleggan paused. "But that can soon change."

"Do I need a lawyer?" he asked, then looked at DS Clark and said, "Can you recommend one?"

She frowned, shook her head. "It would be easier if you could just answer the DCI's question."

"No doubt. Is this about Bunt? Have you found him?"

"We've found a body," Warleggan said. "Get yourself

tidied up and come with us. I can make it official, if you'd prefer. Even get the cuffs out."

Grant hesitated, but he decided not to taunt the man any longer. He wanted answers to his questions too, and he wasn't getting them on the doorstep trading insults.

They gave him five-minutes to wash and change. He took closer to fifteen. When he came back downstairs, DS Clark was in the kitchen and had made coffee. She had tidied up and got rid of the empty bottles too. She looked at him knowingly. He took the coffee and thanked her. He was past embarrassed. Embarrassed was sixty-one days ago when he had woken up in his own piss and vomit. He hadn't known where he was. Enough had been enough and he had vowed to stay dry. Disappointment was today. But disappointment could be beaten. It was only going to take sixty-one days.

"Warleggan is waiting in the car. I thought you might need this first."

"Thanks," he said and took hold of the cup. It had cooled a little in the five-minutes since she had made it and he took a welcome sip.

"So where were you?"

"Looking for Mary," he paused. "Searching for answers in a bottle..."

"Did you find either?"

"No."

She nodded. "Any kind of timescale?"

"I searched for Mary at the manor where I'd last seen her. Then I came back here. I went to the new nursing home where her mother checked in as a resident yesterday. She wasn't there either. I don't know her address, gave up and got back here just after mid-night."

"No alibi?"

"There never is, is there?" he smiled knowingly. "What is happening at Trenvarth Manor? Late night, I take it."

"There's a fire-rescue unit working at the cave. We've drafted in a mountain and cave rescue unit from Wales, but they only got on the scene around four this morning."

"You're wasting your time," he said coldly. "Davey was under the rock. There were tonnes of it. It's a body-recovery operation. Nothing more."

"Well, what should we do? Say a few prayers and lay a wreath? We still retrieve bodies and have a funeral, even in darkest Cornwall," she said, somewhat mockingly. "And while there's a body unaccounted for, we treat it as a rescue until we know otherwise."

Grant shrugged. "Well in that case, tell them to talk to Felicity Roebuck and find out where the entrance to the cave is through the house. It was bricked-up, but they should be three-hundred metres closer if they start at the other end."

She nodded, took out her phone and started to text. "I'm passing that on to the lead officer," she said. "Could have done with that information last night."

"Well, nobody thought to question me." He drank down half the cup then put it down decisively and nodded at her. "Let's go then."

They walked out to the car, where Warleggan was waiting. He was smoking a cigarette and looked impatient. He flicked the stub into the flowerbed and opened the driver's door. "Get in," he said.

"No, I'll follow you in mine."

"Are you not still over the limit?" he asked callously. "You looked to have had a skin full last night."

"You got a breathalyser?"

"I can send for one."

"I thought you were in a rush?"

He seemed to consider this for a moment, then said, "Alright, so be it. There'll be an officer at the crime scene with one, I'm sure."

"Okay, let's go then," Grant said and unlocked his car calling the man's bluff. He was feeling self-destructive. One day it would get the better of him. That's what his shrink had kept telling him. He had fired him, was yet to get a second opinion. He got in, started up and waited for Warleggan and Clark to get into their car.

The sky started to grey over and by the time they drove out of Loe Creek and through Devoran, the clouds were almost black. The rain started soon after and came down in sheets. Grant had the wipers working on full but it wasn't nearly enough. He slowed down, reacting to Warleggan's change of pace, and he dropped back a little more than he usually would. The edges of the road ran like muddy rivers, and the surface water was an inch deep. As they drove through a village called Carnon Downs the covers had blown off storm drains and geysers of brown water sprang at least two feet into the air.

Warleggan drove a complicated route of narrow back-roads and the roads dipped down through two separate valleys. Grant followed carefully and realised from the map on the satnav that they were going to cross the River Fal by ferry and head onto the Roseland Peninsular.

The rain ceased as abruptly as it had started. The clouds remained as grey and heavy and as threatening as they had been before the rainfall, and the landscape fell into a monochrome print. Although the trees were still full of leaves, it looked like a stark winter's day. Grant wondered what a dark February would look like in parts of Cornwall. Part of him hoped he'd never be there to see it.

Grant pulled his car over into the painted waiting lane and watched the ferry make its way slowly across the river. The ferry was asymmetrical with wheelhouse and viewing decks on what Grant would say was the portside but being a ferry on a chain it merely returned without turning. There was a deck wide enough to take three cars abreast and he counted fifteen cars in all. Folded squared-off ramps were hoisted at either end. Through the condensation on his windscreen, he could see the giant chains coming out of the water, threading through great cogs and sprockets. There was an audible clatter, which increased greatly as he lowered his steaming window. The air temperature was still warm for late summer, and combined with the recent deluge of rain, the air steamed and smelled of damp and rotted vegetation. He increased the blowers on the windscreen and the mist cleared quickly. The ferry hit the concrete slipway and the ramp lowered with a mechanical whine. The crew of three worked efficiently and the cars started to disembark and negotiate the steep hill and sharp corner. In a matter of minutes, the queue edged forwards and started up the ramp. Grant was waved forward right up to the bumper of the car in front. He was level with DCI Warleggan and DS Clark. The ramp was raised, and the ferry started on its ten-minute journey across the river. A crew member approached the window with an old-fashioned ticket dispenser and a leather satchel and Grant paid for a return ticket. He glanced at Warleggan, and the man looked away unable to hold his gaze. Grant opened his door and got out. He had noticed a viewing platform and stairs and thought he'd look at the river. The stairs were steel grate and echoed as he climbed them. He saw on old man leaning over the railings and smiled to himself when he realised it was a dummy dressed like a pirate or smuggler.

He walked past and leaned on the railings. He could see the river widening on one side and two enormous cargo vessels on the other which seemed an incredibly unsuitable area for two such ships.

"They keep ships up here that need working on in Falmouth docks." He turned and saw DS Clark standing just a few feet away. "That, or when the crew have difficulties to resolve. A ship stayed here for three months because of industrial action. Another because the company could not pay the port fees and were going into receivership. During the Covid Pandemic there were quite a few ships anchored up wherever it was deep enough."

Grant nodded. "Must be deep water here."

"One of the deepest channels in the world. I think Falmouth is the deepest natural harbour. Or second deepest," she paused. "Shit, it's pretty deep, whatever..."

Grant chuckled. "So that's the Carrick Roads, out there?" He pointed to the widening river.

"Yes."

"So, the Pandora Inn where we ate is down that way?"

She nodded, stepped in closer and leaned against the railing next to him. "It's down that way, then back up another creek. There's a quite few creeks on the water."

"Warleggan still doesn't like me much, does he," he stated flatly. "He thinks I've killed Pete Bunt."

"No," she paused. "He doesn't like you, no. But he doesn't think you killed Bunt."

Grant relaxed a little. He looked up and saw how close they were to the slipway. The water looked black and unimaginably deep, the sky was still as foreboding and threatened to empty itself imminently. He realised they were almost across the river and said, "We'd better be getting back."

The ramp scraped the concrete slipway and the gates opened. The cars had all long since started their engines and when the crew member started to wave the lanes of vehicles off it was like the start of a race. Grant took his cue and disembarked. Warleggan was now behind him, and he drove a way up the steep road, then pulled in and waited for him to pass. Once he had, Grant tucked in behind and followed him out of the valley. The road was fast, but most Cornish roads seemed to be. The traffic kept to ten miles an hour slower than a three-lane motorway, but on a road with only a car and a half's width at most times. Pull ins had been cut into the hedges every fifty or sixty metres, so Cornish drivers would no doubt be adept at reversing as well as rally racing.

They followed the road to Gerrans and Portscatho but turned off shortly before. The road became even narrower and before long Grant caught a glimpse of the sea. It was difficult to tell the blackness of the sea from the sky. The road dropped downhill and swept to the right. There was a slipway for launching small boats on the left and a sandy carpark on the right. Two police cars were parked as a barrier with one police officer sitting in one of the vehicles talking on the radio and three police officers milling around and chatting. They seemed to jump to it when they saw DCI Warleggan, but it was an isolated posting on a quiet morning. There was only so much busy work that could be done. Before the two cars parked, they had reverted to chatting amongst themselves.

Large boulders lay scattered on the beach and the first third of the beach was made up almost entirely from pebbles and rocks, then gradually it turned to sand all the way down to the low-tide mark. Grant parked alongside Warleggan and got out of the Alfa Romeo. He looked at DS

Clark as she got out. She shivered, but it wasn't cold. She saw him looking and said, "I don't like this place much," she paused. "There were three fishermen gunned down here one night, a while ago now. A smuggling venture gone wrong."

"Or gone right," Grant said. "Depending on your point of view. It obviously worked out for someone."

"You've got all the smart answers, haven't you," Warleggan sneered. He pulled on an anorak over his suit. It wasn't raining, but it was merely a matter of time. "Come on." He strode out across the sandy carpark and headed for the police officers stationed on the carpark entrance.

Grant was surprised at the speed at which the detective walked. DS Clark started to jog alongside. "No, he definitely still doesn't like you," she whispered.

Warleggan spoke to the uniformed officers briefly, nodded, then looked back at them as they approached. "The coroner and SOCO are on the way to do a preliminary. They'll be here before mid-tide," he paused. "Before it's a problem, at least. This way," he said curtly.

Grant looked out to sea. There was a thin sliver of grey between the blackness of the sky and the blackness mirrored by the Atlantic. White horses tossed all the way to the horizon. There were only three fishing vessels several miles out. Nobody went to sea on days like these unless their livelihoods *really* depended on it. The beach was deserted. There was no real colour to it, merely the complete spectrum of grey in this monochrome scene. The rain started to fall again, heavy but by no means like the earlier deluge.

Grant noticed the pile of red in the middle of the beach. The colour emphasised by both the darkness of the sky and the sea and the emptiness of the waterlogged beach. His mind took a moment to take it in, then the realisation dawned. He jumped down off the ledge and onto the pebbles. Running on them was difficult, but it became easier as the terrain went through to shale and then wet sand. His heart raced, but only from knowing what he would find, and not from uncertainty or hope. The red gave way to pale skin tones and the long locks of amber hair, wet and matted, draped over her shoulders and the wet sand.

He slowed, walked the last few paces, rounding the body until he could see the eyes, staring out across the wet sand. Mary's once glossy and alert eyes looked dull and indifferent. Her skin had always been pale but had now whitened and shone with a sheen of seawater. Her red dress was soaked, becoming almost see through, but even from where he stood, Grant could see she wore no underwear underneath. He had snatched glimpses of a red bra under her dress last night and a faint knicker line as she had climbed the stairs.

He looked at both Clark and Warleggan as they approached. "Has anybody disturbed the body?"

"It's been in the sea," Warleggan said. "There won't be any DNA."

"*She*, not it!" Grant corrected him savagely.

"There could still be DNA internally," Clark commented. "If anybody... interfered with her..."

Grant glanced down at Mary's body, then looked back at DCI Warleggan. "I thought you wanted to speak to me regarding Pete Bunt..."

Warleggan shrugged. "Don't know where you got that idea."

"So where *is* Pete Bunt?"

"No idea," Warleggan paused. "But it looks like he left a little parting gift for you. Turn her over..."

"Why?" Grant asked.

Warleggan stared at him, nodded towards the body. "Just do it."

"I'm not falling for it," Grant said coldly. "I'm not touching a body after you asked me for an alibi for last night..."

"You're not under suspicion," DS Clark interjected.

"So why the hell bring me out here? You inferred that the body would be Bunt's. You asked me for an alibi. What sort of crap are you peddling here?"

"Fine! I'll do it!" Warleggan bent down and grabbed hold of a handful of her red hair and pulled. He put his toe under her shoulder to lever her up.

Grant kicked Warleggan in his buttocks, as much as a shove as a kick, and the man went sprawling into the wet sand. "Show some fucking respect!" he snapped. He knelt in the sand and carefully eased his left hand under her waist and his right hand under her shoulder. She was ice cold, wet and sandy. Rigor mortis was starting to set in. There was a finality to it, more so than just seeing her body and knowing that she was dead. It was a macabre confirmation. He eased her over into the recovery position, her head did not flop back when he let her go, she was stiffening quickly. He stood back and stared at her bare back. He took in the tiny dolphin tattoo he had seen, had found somewhat erotic when she had turned up with the takeaway.

"Do you see?" Warleggan said from behind him. He brushed the sand off his clothes and stood back. He didn't look happy, but he didn't square up to Grant either. He seemed to take the fall, but he seemed smug too, like he was looking forward to something else to come. "You see what coming down here and poking about has done, where it has got you?"

The bleeding had long-since stopped and the sea had washed any blood away. The knife wounds were deep, cut at least an inch into her pallor flesh, the red of the muscle exposed and looking like veal steaks. Grant had no trouble reading the message. He felt bile rise in his throat as he read.

Grant - she's all yours now. It must have taken him ages to carve the lettering into her soft flesh. Grant hoped she had been dead at the time, but he doubted it. God, he needed another drink...

"So, why did you bring me out here?" Grant asked quietly, staring at the words etched deep into her body. "You could have told me about this back at the house."

Warleggan sneered at him. "You come down here, telling us what to do, with no authority and a letter you forged, just to give you credibility. Some hot-shot anti-terrorism officer with a medal you didn't deserve. Everybody knows you drowned that terrorist, even if it couldn't be proved..." He paused, his sneer turning to a look of pure loathing. "You treat me like some fucking security guard, not a DCI with twenty-years on the job. Well, here it is. This is what happened because you stirred up a load of shit and..."

Warleggan didn't finish the sentence. And nor did he see the punch coming. He was out cold and heading towards the sand. Grant was already walking away and called to Clark without looking back, "You might want to turn that piece of shit over before he becomes the second body on this shitty beach."

Chapter Thirty-Four

Grant had driven to Camborne police station and after he had convinced the custody sergeant to let him in, he found DS Jago in the CID suite. The detective sergeant had called social services who had located temporary housing for the family. They were indeed Syrian, and their family name was Nassir. They had travelled for eleven months and lost the maternal grandmother on the way to a harsh winter and chronic asthma. They had what was left of their savings stolen in France. They had been approached in Calais and offered safe passage to England in return for work. In return for this, they were to be obligated for three months, then given jobs and paid in accordance with British law. It seemed like a good deal. They had been promised agricultural work. But that wasn't what happened to the Hafeez family. Their story had been very different indeed, and Grant knew that the Nassir's would not have been treated any differently. Especially as the family identified the criminal record photograph that Grant had showed them as Pete Bunt, the man who had approached them in Calais, and one of the men who had transported them across the channel, down the south coast of England and all the way up the creek to the jetty opposite Loe Creek. Grant had printed off a photograph from John Pascoe's social media account and the family had identified him as the second man on the boat.

They had been lucky, and when Grant met up with them in St. Austell, they showed their gratitude in a series of hugs and thanks, from broken English spoken by the parents to the middle eastern Kardashian of the daughters. Grant had been quite overwhelmed by their sincerity and appreciation, and the little girl had cried when she had been reunited with her lost teddy bear. She had hugged him warmly, and for a moment Grant had been taken back to a happier time when he would have a cuddle with Chloe on those rare evenings when he got home early enough. He hadn't realised how precious those moments had been until they were gone.

He had bid them farewell, then driven on to Truro. He had wanted to deliver the news of Mary's death to her mother. He hadn't wanted DS Clark, with her judgemental views of the woman, nor DCI Warleggan to be the bearers of something so monumental. He had not known Mary for very long, but he felt he had a real connection. He had liked her, been attracted to her, and when he had discovered her story, her reasoning for what she had been forced to do, he had helped her all he could. But ultimately, he wanted to be the one to tell her mother, because he had not been there for Mary at the end. He had asked her to wait outside of Roebuck's study and that had been the last time he had seen her alive. He needed a penance. He needed to make amends. The ninth step. His path through alcohol recovery had been unchallenged at this step, this essential part of the process. He was starting on the road again, surely the final time, and he needed to take every single step this time. The ninth was the hardest of all. Had he not turned to the bottle after leaving Trenvarth Manor, he may well have found Mary. May have been able to save her.

Emily Hocking had not taken the news well. She had yet to settle into the new residential home. Now there was grief and disbelief at the news, as well as the uncertainty of her new surroundings. He had spent an hour with her, hearing stories about Mary's childhood, passing tissues, comforting her and explaining that the end had been swift. He knew, of course, that it hadn't been. It had been anything but. He could see for himself that her underwear had been removed and that it was likely Bunt had raped her. It was more than likely she had been alive when the words had been cut into her, because drowning was Bunt's proven method of killing. He suspected that the same method had been used to drown her as the entire Hafeez family, and John Trevithick just for being in the wrong place at the wrong time. Bunt would have chosen the beach after rounding St Anthony Head on the Roseland Peninsular, as he escaped in his fishing vessel. He could be anywhere now, berthed in a quiet cove or creek, or perhaps even in France. He would have a knowledge of the French coastline if he had successfully brought in illegal immigrants.

Grant had looked for a carer to sit with Emily and taken his leave. He felt awful. Awful enough for a drink? No doubt. But today was day one, and he was sure he would make it this time.

He had packed his bag and dropped it in the doorway to the lounge. He would have to give the keys back to Maitland's wife when he returned to London. There would be the funeral, too. It suddenly struck him that in the whirlwind since finding out about Maitland's battle with cancer and his death and watching the boat moor on the jetty across the creek, he had not had a moment to grieve. Maybe Maitland would have wanted it like that. Perhaps that was why he had sent Grant down under the guise of recovery, then sent him the file. Grant certainly liked the thought of that.

He picked up his jacket, then frowned at the weight. The pocket. He fished out the mobile phone. John Pascoe's mobile phone. There was little battery left, but the screen indicated several missed calls and texts. Grant thumbed through as he made his way to his bag and took his charger out of the side pocket. He wanted to get some charge into it before it switched off. It was an iPhone, and many were set up to require a thumbprint upon restarting. Pascoe hadn't had a screen lock code installed, but even so, everyone set up their phone differently.

Plugged in and charging, Grant looked at the numbers, the names and the times and dates of the calls and texts. He looked at the screen thoughtfully, then started to compose a reply to the last text it had received.

Chapter Thirty-Five

Grant watched the car turn a wide circle, its headlights cutting a swathe of light through the darkness like a lighthouse through a thick sea-mist. The driver parked nose out. It was a professional thing to do. You could get out of trouble a lot faster that way.

Grant had driven up earlier, parked in a field after battling to open the gate. His car was next to the hedge, unseen from the track. He hadn't responded to the text. He had the bait on the hook and a nibble had been taken. He needed to tease until he got a real bite. In this case, doing nothing was everything.

The driver switched off the engine and the lights went out after thirty-seconds. Courtesy lights to get you into your house. Grant remained where he was. He watched, waited. The car was parked twenty feet from the edge of the abyss. Nobody goes that close to the abyss without looking down at it. It was a morbid human fascination. Like the people who had parked and walked across the road at Hell's Mouth. Grant had done the same thing. Sure enough, after a minute or so, the door opened, and the driver got out. The half-moon illuminated them. Grant made his move. He climbed up the hedge, swung his leg over and slid down the other side. He pushed himself out from the hedge and stepped up out of the ditch. He was twenty metres away.

"You should have moved the for rent sign," he said.

DS Lucy Clark spun around, squinted at him in the darkness, her eyes were not yet accustomed to the dark. "What do you mean? What are *you* doing here, Grant?"

"Back at that executive new-build in Porthtowan," he said. "The house had a for rent sign from Keith and Davey. The sign had been taken down and stored by the side of the house. The same estate agents as the houses that Mary was working out of both in Loe Creek and Portreath. The same Keith Davey who was up to his neck in the illegal trafficking and imprisonment of people for the sex-slave trade."

"I just got the keys to that house to meet you somewhere safe and private," she said defensively.

"I went into more than just the bathroom," he paused. "There was a room geared up for accepting clients. It was a working brothel. You said the house was part of an investigation, but nothing had been tagged or logged. No evidence had been removed."

"You'll have to do better than that!" she scoffed. "What exactly are you accusing me of?"

"I don't buy that you had a call to get back to the station. I don't think you wrote me a note and I'm sure your phone records will prove there was never a call. So, what was meant to have happened? John Pascoe enters the house as you leave and attacks me? Binds my hands and drives me up here?"

"What the hell has John Pascoe got to do with this?"

"You tell me," he replied. "You're up here tonight because of the text from his phone."

"So?"

"He's the third man in this endeavour. He's a lawyer."

"And?"

"You had a lawyer boyfriend. You clashed in court. You said you left him because he got a man off a rape charge," Grant said. "That man was Pete Bunt. That lawyer was John Pascoe. I've checked. It isn't difficult to do."

"It's a small county. Coincidence is a daily occurrence."

"I asked around, spoke to some of your team. DS Jago in particular. He said you and John Pascoe were still very much an on and off item."

"Fuck buddy, so what?" she said flippantly. "I'm up here responding to his text. A woman has needs."

"Pascoe was up to his neck in all of this. He has been identified as one of the men who brought the Nassir's into the country. His work schedule will confirm he was absent at the time. I bet that it will do the same around the time of the Hafeez family's deaths. I'm also willing to bet he was stupid enough to carry his mobile phone at the time. It's as good as a tracking device. You know that I could get a map reading from its GPS. It will show exactly where he has been and what route he took..."

"Nothing to do with me. No connection."

"When we went back to Camborne's CID suite for you to sort out the request for the exhumation, you were being really *friendly* with me."

"It was a friendly kind of day!" She smiled, cocked her head. "I seem to remember you asking for a date."

Grant shrugged. "I do a lot that I later regret," he paused. "DS Jago slipped his jacket on and left abruptly. I thought he was pissed off that you were helping the stranger in the camp, that he was loyal to DCI Warleggan. He just thought you were working another angle. He is in line for

detective inspector, as are you. As usual, there's two quali-
fied officers, but only one post up for grabs. He feels that
you have an unfair advantage. You are the golden girl. Not
because of your abilities as a police officer. But because of
your one time, on and off, two-year affair with DCI Warleggan. Nobody's meant to know, but like in most workplaces,
everybody does."

"It happens. You end up working a lot of hours, the
same hours..."

"I thought Warleggan was involved. I thought that he
blocked Hastings, Adams and Jago and called for no further
action. But you had the man's ear. Not only did he want to
continue massaging both his ego and other things with a far
younger, attractive woman, but he was desperate for his
wife not to find out about his affair. He has two young teens,
doesn't want his family pulled apart. You were his
puppeteer, through nothing more than sex and a few calculated, but casual-sounding conversations on how it could
pan out for him if he didn't listen to you. You controlled
him, and with that, the angle from within the police.
Guided by Pascoe, or maybe you even guided *him*..." He
shook his head. "No, I know you guided him. *Guided* them
all. You played me too, all the little flirtations, I was just a
fool to believe you would be interested. And today, on the
beach, Warleggan said that there would be no DNA after
exposure to the seawater, but it was *you* who said that it
could still be there internally. That was the whole reason
for digging up the Hafeez family. You felt that if it were
investigated, which would only be a matter of time, then the
DNA of whoever had sex with them... *raped* them, would
create a trail. Sooner or later there would be a match and it
would all come crashing down. You got lucky with the racial
tension thing, the Islamic community insisting they were

properly buried. It made an open and shut case shut far more quickly."

She shrugged. "So now what? Are you recording this?"

He shook his head. "No. Not this time."

"So, what do you want? Money?" she asked. "Everyone want's money."

"Not everyone."

"Then they're stupid. There's more than enough money to change your life forever. I can get you a quarter of a million tonight. Just to keep quiet and walk away. Think about it; that's a hell of an amount of money. If you want in, you could take on a role in London. There are filthy immigrants on every street up there. They're all over the place. You could send them down our way. You could earn that much again in another six months. Half a million a year, no problem. I have, and I've stashed it away." She paused, looking at him curiously. "How in the hell did you get John's phone?"

"You followed him when he drove me up here, didn't you," he said accusingly. "You took him back for his car."

"I knew he'd pussy out," she said. "I should have stayed and helped him. You cut him a deal, didn't you? The spineless piece of shit. They're all the same, lawyers. So, will he turn Queen's evidence? Cut a deal for immunity?"

"There was no deal."

"So where did he get to?"

Grant stepped closer to her, and she stepped back a pace. She was no more than four feet from the edge. "He was going to get me into my car and send it over the edge. You planned it with him. You helped him by driving him back for his car. So what? You didn't want to get your own hands dirty?"

"That bastard," she said coldly. "So, he confessed and gave you the phone. Then what?"

Grant tossed her Pascoe's phone and she caught it. It was reactionary and she looked at the screen. He shook his head. "No. He took my place," he said. "After I killed him, kicked the life out of him, I strapped him into his Porsche and gave it a little bump over the edge with my own car."

"You *killed* him?" she looked at him disbelievingly. "Bullshit! You wouldn't do that!"

"You don't know me at all..."

"Oh, I think I do," she sneered. "You're a fucking boy scout! You're all about what's right and wrong!"

"I'm all about sticking up for people who can't. I'm all about justice, yes. But I can ignore the law's definition of right or wrong if I have to."

"So, you did drown that terrorist..."

He nodded. "One less to worry about."

She cocked her head and stared incredulously. "Seriously, you killed John Pascoe?"

"He's right below you."

She looked like she did not know whether to laugh or cry. "You murdered him! Well, that ties you in now. We're both the wrong side of the law," she said, then smiled. "Well perhaps now, we cancel each other out..."

Grant took a step forward and shoved her hard in her chest. She staggered backwards, her face not comprehending what he had done, but as her feet found no purchase and she reached the edge, her eyes went wide, and she stared at Grant in ominous realisation. She did not scream. Most people who fell from a great height never made a sound and Lucy Clark was no different. But to Grant, the silence of her fall was worse than he imagined. Ominous and final.

Chapter Thirty-Six

One week later
London

Grant wasn't a lover of religion, but he would have to admit that he found churches to be a calm, contemplative place to spend time. There was a serenity that he found difficult to describe. The same went with graveyards. Perhaps there was an acceptance that eventually, even if you lived your life without religion, you ended up somewhere like this. The proximity to death made one contemplate life, and while doing so, with the knowledge that we are here for such a short time, serenity is easily reached. It wasn't something you could fight against and win. Ultimately, there really was only one conclusion for all.

The graveyard was neatly kept, the grass cut short, and the bushes and shrubs trimmed and shaped to keep the path free for people to walk two-abreast, as was common practice when walking to burial plots, behind a coffin carried by six.

He had missed the funeral. He had at least wanted to hear Maitland's eulogy, but he had been assured by those he knew in attendance that it was, at the same time, both fitting and utter bullshit. A parody that so many knew so little about the man, and so few knew little more. There were anecdotes told that his colleagues knew nothing of, and untold anecdotes his colleagues dare not divulge to his family. A life of almost thirty-years in the police service, with twenty of those years spent in the fight against terrorism had left its mark. Maitland was both a larger-than-life character and a shadow, depending on who you asked.

The investigation into DS Clark's involvement with John Pascoe was ongoing. Quite how or why events had led them both to the precipice was unclear. Their bodies had both been recovered, as had Clark's vehicle. Her body had washed up on Perranporth Beach, further up the tidal current, and Pascoe's car had been spotted by an ornithologist at low tide. Just enough shadow for the man, familiar to the location in his search for Cornish choughs, to know there was an anomaly. A search and rescue team had recovered his body, but any recovery of the vehicle looked unlikely because of the sheer logistics involved. Phone records had shown multiple texts and calls between Clark and Pascoe, and vast stashes of cash had been found at both their addresses and at Pascoe's offices in Truro. Officers had been drafted down from Exeter to lead the investigation and DCI Warleggan had been taken off the case, with his rank of DCI under review. Pete Bunt was still at large and subject to an active UK manhunt as well as being placed on Interpol's watch list wanted for multiple murders, people trafficking, false imprisonment and sexual assault including rape.

As for the Hafeez family, their bodies were still missing.

Pete Bunt was the only person who could perhaps one day shed light on their final resting place. With thousands of unmapped mineshafts and ventilation shafts across the county, long claimed by nature, there really wasn't a place to start.

Grant hadn't brought flowers with him. He imagined there would have been enough already, and besides, Maitland would have ribbed him terribly about giving another man flowers. He had found the grave easily enough. Freshly dug and filled with loose earth piled in a slight mound, the headstone newly polished and seated perfectly upright. The headstone was, however, non-descript. There were black marble affairs, with white or gold inlaid writing, that seemed to be a popular choice, but either Maitland had left instructions, or his wife had chosen an austere stone that looked like slate to Grant. The engraving was deep and in a relatively plain font. Nothing flamboyant, nothing to indicate that a good man rested here, a man who had gone over and above for the security of his country.

Grant sat back on the bench. Some of the trees were starting to shed their leaves and even though he was only three-hundred miles east and a hundred miles north of Cornwall, he had felt a chill upon returning. The summer was finally over and like so many things in his life, he would be glad to lay it to rest and move on.

"Are you here for Commander Maitland?" The quiet voice belonged to a man who sounded wholly respectful of Grant's solitude.

In his unguarded and sombre state, Grant had been startled by the voice behind him and flinched. He turned and saw a gentle-looking man in his sixties. He wore a dog collar and a black shirt and had taken to a grey cardigan to beat the chill. Maitland had been Church of England so this would make the man a vicar, or at least Grant assumed so. "I am," he replied. "I missed the ceremony and wanted to come and pay my respects."

"Funeral, my son," the vicar smiled. "Ceremonies are for weddings..." There was no condescension in his tone.

"Fair enough."

"Are you a family member? I could say a few words if you'd like?"

Grant shook his head. "No, I'm not. And no, that's okay, thanks."

"A colleague?"

"Yes."

"And a member?"

Grant frowned. "Sorry?"

"Not member, no. I mean a fellow brother."

"Brother?"

"Yes," the vicar said. "There was a good showing, a ceremonial reading afterwards from his brothers at the lodge." He looked at Grant, then added, "The freemasons..."

Grant got up off the bench and walked over to the grave. He looked at the headstone. At the top, in the centre of the stone, above the name was an emblem, an insignia. A setsquare forming a vee at the bottom and a pair of compasses inverted over a letter G. There were no accompanying words. It was small and he had mistaken it for a rose or something similar.

Grant thought about what Mary had said about John Pascoe. A freemason from a family of freemasons. Keith Davey's handshake. Grant had confronted him about it, taunted him even, in Trenvarth Manor at the charity event. It was how he had been able to break the man's finger so easily.

Had Maitland known? Had they approached him, a

fellow mason? Asked him to help them in their sickening endeavour? What had sparked Maitland to have his inkling about the deaths of the Hafeez family? How did he know there was going to be more people trafficked? He had marked the dates and times of the high tides for Grant to keep a lookout. And why had he not briefed Grant thoroughly, given him a clear path to follow, rather than instructions to start at the beginning and see what he could turn up? Would he have felt torn between justice and the idea of turning against his fellow brethren?

"You'll know when you see it, son. It will all become clear. And I trust that you will know what to do..." Those had been Maitland's final words to Grant.

Grant looked down at the headstone. He had a lump in his throat and a tear was welling in his eye and he said quietly, "I see it now, Sir..." He paused. "I know what I did wasn't lawful. I'm not even sure it was right, but I hope I did what needed to be done..."

Author's Note

Author's Note

Thanks for making it this far and I hope you enjoyed reading the story as much as I enjoyed writing it!

If you would like to read more of my work, you can find it here: www.apbateman.com where there are buying links, further information and a sign-up for my newsletter (you get a free novella just for signing up!) As usual, I would be grateful if you could leave a short review on Amazon, or just click the star rating. It all helps to keep my writing visible.

Well, thanks, and I hope to entertain you again soon.

A P Bateman

Printed in Great Britain
by Amazon

28291183R00145